THE SOUL S(

by Geoffrey Sleight

To Tom and Katie

CHAPTER 1

THE FIRST two weeks in their new home were the happiest times for Paul Hunter and his family. After that, events descended into a nightmare.

Paul was an architect and had slogged dutifully as an employee of a large corporate for 16 years since qualifying in his mid twenties.

The move was part of his plan to set up as a freelance, and gradually build a business in his own right.

Of course, he had no idea of what awaited.

His wife, Diane, was an experienced public relations consultant. She too had worked for a large organisation, and also had plans to form a business.

But first she would spend time re-organising the house to suit the style the couple desired, including structural alterations. And, more importantly, help their daughters, Alice 11 and Rosemary 14, settle into their new surroundings and the local school.

The house was a large, four-bedroomed property beside a quiet leafy lane in the village of Lynthorne. A considerable step-up from the small, three-bed semi where they had lived, forty miles away, in a traffic-clogged suburb of outer London.

The sisters had been reluctant to move at first, leaving behind friends, but soon adapted to enjoy the benefits of beautiful, open countryside on their doorstep.

The first two weeks of happiness, however, came to an abrupt end one night, when the girls were sharing a bedroom while re-decoration in the house took place.

Rosemary, the older sister, had not been able to sleep well that night. She was having strange dreams in which bizarre figures were trying to steal something precious from her. She awoke, feeling uneasy. In the dimness of a night light on the chest of drawers, she saw an elderly man and woman standing at the foot of the bed, staring at her.

For a moment she was frozen in terror. Then she calmed down, thinking perhaps the couple had lost their way and wandered into the house by mistake.

"Are you lost?" she asked. They continued to stare at her, looking troubled as if they were seeing some portent of ill fortune.

Rosemary's voice woke her sister Alice, sleeping in the bed beside. She looked up and, seeing the couple, screamed.

Paul and Diane shot bolt upright in bed, awoken by the piercing sound. In seconds they had crossed the bedroom, and were speeding down the landing to their daughters' room. Alice was crying, terrified by what she'd seen.

"There were ghosts in our room," she insisted as her parents attempted to comfort her.

"You've had a bad dream, that's all," Diane reassured her.

"But it was an old man and woman. They were staring at us," Alice would not be placated.

Paul turned to Rosemary.

"Tell Alice it was a dream," he felt sure confirmation from her sister would calm the girl.

But Rosemary was looking pale. She remained silent for a moment.

"I saw them too," she replied, quietly. "And now they're not here."

Paul and Diane searched round the room and then the house, wondering if an elderly couple had found their way into the property. But no-one else was present. All the entry doors and windows were locked.

For the remainder of the night the girls slept with their mother, and Paul stayed in the girls' bedroom. As daylight broke, no further disturbance had occurred.

Both girls still looked shaken as they sat half-heartedly eating their breakfast. Diane was concerned and suggested they stay off school for the day. But their desire was to get out of the house for a while.

"I'm sure you didn't actually see ghosts," their mother tried to reassure them as she made a coffee. "Sometimes

3

dim lighting can make things in a room look like something else for a moment."

Her daughters looked unconvinced.

"We both saw them!" they replied.

"Then they were gone. They disappeared into thin air," added Alice. "This place is haunted."

Diane didn't reply. Youngsters had vivid imaginations. She could offer no rational explanation for what they believed they had seen. But she was certain it was nothing supernatural.

"I'm not sleeping in that room again," Alice insisted, as she rose from the kitchen table to collect her school bag.

"Nor am I," Rosemary agreed, joining her sister.

"Well, daddy and I will move into your room and you can both sleep in ours," Diane offered a solution. The girls settled with the offer.

As Diane was leaving to drive them both to school, Paul appeared at the top of the stairs. He'd been on the phone in his makeshift office, talking to a new client.

"Have a good day girls," he called to them, "and don't worry. There's no such thing as ghosts."

His daughters said nothing, and left the house with their mother.

On Diane's return, Paul came down from his office to have coffee and chat with her in the living room. They sat on the sofa amid a setting of chairs, tables, dressers and lamps, which still hadn't found their rightful place in the house while re-decoration was continuing.

"I'm worried about the girls," Diane voiced her thoughts.

"It's a new home for them. Youngsters imagine all sorts of things," Paul sat forward on the sofa, clasping the coffee mug in his hands to warm them."

"But they couldn't both have seen these..." Diane hesitated to find the right word, "...people."

"One of them thinks they see something and describes it to the other. Next moment they have both 'seen' or imagined it too," her husband gave his explanation of the strange visitors in the girls' bedroom. "Kids just have over-active imaginations. I did. Can't believe you didn't too."

His wife didn't disagree, but still appeared doubtful.

Paul place his mug on the coffee table beside him.

"You're not telling me that you actually believe in ghosts?" he asked, incredulously turning to face her.

Diane sipped her coffee, looking thoughtful.

"Well...no," she paused. She was an educated woman. Belief in supernatural beings seemed primitive, something that was understandable as a belief in earlier times, but didn't fit with the sophisticated, modern world.

"No, I don't believe in ghosts," she hesitated.

"But perhaps something dreadful happened to someone here. Perhaps they leave some sort of energy behind, something that manifests itself in a way we don't yet understand. That someday science will be able to explain."

Diane wasn't sure if she'd convinced herself with the explanation, let alone her husband.

He stared at her, shaking his head in disbelief.

"Well, in all the years we've been married, I never thought you believed in spirits and all that hokum."

"I don't," she protested. "You misunderstand."

"What dreadful thing do you think has happened here?" Paul asked.

"I don't know." His wife looked confused.

They decided to leave it at that, and discuss instead how they could best help the children restore the happiness they'd enjoyed in their new home until the previous night.

For the next few nights all was peaceful, the manifestation seemed to have ceased. Then the couple were awoken by a piercing scream in the early hours, coming from the bedroom they'd swapped with the girls.

They ran to see what was wrong and found their daughters hugging each other, looking terrified.

"What's happened?" Their parents were fraught.

"We saw them again!" Rosemary struggled to speak, shaking.

"They were standing by the bed, looking down at us as if they were trying to tell us something."

6

"All right, it's all right. We won't leave you alone at night again," Diane cuddled them.

"We'll find out what's going on. Ghosts don't really exist. Perhaps something or someone is playing a nasty trick," their mother tried to offer a rational explanation.

"What did they look like?" their father wondered if a description might be valuable to the police. It was possible intruders may have somehow gained entry.

The girls were too confused to offer any useful description, except Rosemary had noted the man had a large, red birthmark on his left cheek.

Diane slept in the room with them for the rest of the night.

Next day, Paul left the house to see a client. Diane took the children to school then returned home, wondering how she could get to the bottom of the strange appearances the girls had seen.

She made a coffee in the kitchen. Her thoughts also touched on the spare bedroom upstairs where she had plans to set up an office and start her own public relations business. She needed to keep focussed on that as well.

Paul had lost a sizeable income leaving his company to branch out and build a business of his own. In the meantime, she would need to help boost their funds.

Diane left the kitchen, carrying her coffee, to make her way upstairs and look over the bedroom which would be her future office. She was still deciding where the desk and equipment would be best placed. She hadn't made a final decision.

At the bottom of the staircase she looked up. Standing on the landing she saw an elderly man and woman gazing down at her.

She leapt back in fear, dropping the coffee mug, which shattered spreading the contents across the tiled hallway. When she looked up again, no-one was there.

Diane rang her husband and told him what had happened.

"I'm in the middle of an important meeting. I can't discuss it now," he sounded impatient. "This business has made you all start to imagine things. I'll get back as soon as I can." He hung up.

Diane was beginning to think he was right, but she was reluctant to go upstairs on her own. She felt silly. A grown woman afraid of...imaginings. But if it was imagination, it held a powerful grip. After spending time reasoning that it may well have been just her imagination she went upstairs, cautiously, fearful that any second the old couple might appear. All the rooms were empty. But the emptiness echoed a sense of foreboding.

The next couple of nights once again passed peacefully. Paul, for the reassurance of his family, now slept on his own in a single bed, while Diane stayed in the other bedroom with the girls. It was becoming ridiculous, he thought. He really must find out who was causing this charade so normal life could be restored.

He was becoming convinced there was a secret entry into the house and some neighbours, for whatever reason, were playing unacceptable pranks. Ghosts did not exist. Of that he was absolutely certain.

When yet another night passed without disturbance, Paul began to think the drama was over.

His hope was short lived.

At breakfast, Alice was eating her cereal with her sister and parents at the kitchen table.

"Why were you arguing last night?" she suddenly posed the question to her mother and father.

They looked at each other quizzically.

"We weren't arguing last night," Diane replied.

"I heard you," the child insisted. "I woke up in the middle of the night and you weren't in the bedroom," she looked at her mother. "You were downstairs arguing with daddy."

Diane and Paul were totally baffled. They'd both gone to bed at the same time and hadn't left the room all night. Certainly they hadn't been arguing.

"You were saying something like 'he'll be the finish of us all,'" Alice looked at her father.

"And you said 'just leave him alone,'" the girl turned to her mother.

"Who were you talking about?"

"I think you must have been dreaming, darling," Diane had absolutely no idea what her daughter was talking about, but like her husband, was beginning to wonder if the house was starting to cause their daughters psychological problems.

Alice's older sister, Rosemary, was not aware of anyone arguing in the night, but her feeling of unease was plain to see.

Diane took the children to school and returned to the house. Her husband was out again meeting a client.

Her original feeling of happiness in the new home had dissolved and was now replaced with apprehension. She feared seeing the appearance of the old couple again and kept looking behind, wondering if they were standing there, watching her.

She told herself to get a grip. It would be intolerable to continually live in a state of fear. Spirits did not exist her rational self insisted. But deep in her primeval psyche, dread of the unknown ruled.

She walked into the kitchen to make a coffee when the doorbell rang. It was the postman delivering a parcel. She'd ordered a necklace and opened the package in the hallway, examining the jewellery, then trying it on to see if she liked it in the reflection of the hall mirror.

Satisfied with the purchase, she returned to the kitchen to make the coffee. Her eyes caught sight of a carving knife laying on the counter beside the knife-block. Her mouth dropped in horror. She hadn't removed it from the block. Of that she was certain. Or was she?

Perhaps she had, absent-mindedly. But she would have remembered. Or perhaps someone or something else had removed it. The knife wasn't on the counter when she'd left the kitchen to answer the postman's call. A chill ran through her. Was it those...?

Diane wondered if she should ring her husband. It would sound pathetic. A grown woman letting her fear run away with her. But the children were suffering. This house was not good. She rang Paul and told him about the knife. As expected, he wasn't sympathetic.

"You obviously put it there without remembering. You're always putting things somewhere then forgetting where you've put them. This business is getting out of hand." His frustration at the disruption of family life was getting to him.

"Just try and relax. I'll talk to you when I get home this evening."

"I'm not spending another night in this house," Diane decided to put her foot down.

"The children are suffering and I won't let it go on. I'm taking them to stay with my parents for a while."

Paul was silent for a moment.

"Look, can we talk about this when I get back? It shouldn't be too late."

Diane agreed, but she didn't plan to hang around for long.

When her husband returned, he saw two suitcases in the hallway. Diane and the children were wearing their coats, waiting to leave. Paul became angry, slamming his briefcase down on the floor.

"You can't just leave like this," he shouted. "What about their education?" He pointed toward the children.

"They don't want to stay here. They're not going to learn much frightened out of their wits," Diane replied. "I'll find another school."

Paul's anger melted into sorrow.

"We had such plans. What about them?"

"We'll have to work something out," Diane offered a compromise.

"These apparitions, they're just imagination. Can't you see that?" Paul pleaded.

"That may be. But they're very real to us. We're not staying here." Diane was unmoved.

"We'll sell the house. Find somewhere else," Paul bargained. "Will that make you happy. Will you stay until then?"

Diane agreed with selling the house, but adamant she and children would live with her parents in the meantime.

"But their house is sixty miles away in Bridgeworth. I can't work here and visit you every day. It will have to be weekends." Paul was deeply upset at the prospect of being parted in this way.

Diane and the girls were also extremely sad to be separated from their father. But relieved at not spending another night in the house.

Paul hadn't experienced the strange activities his family had encountered. It was difficult for him to understand a problem which, for him, did not exist other than in their minds. He kissed them, and with a heavy heart, watched them leave.

That night he decided to sleep in the main bedroom, where he'd originally slept with his wife before his daughters' nightmares had started. Nightmares. Unreal phantoms. That was his simple explanation for their unfounded fears.

He felt very lonely. Only a few weeks ago the house had rung with happiness. Now the silence in the absence of his family seemed to hang heavily in the air.

He climbed into bed and turned off the bedside light, laying still, wondering what he could do to make his wife and daughters feel comfortable in the house again. He was reluctant to sell so soon. Only a short time ago, it was going to be the location of a fresh, new start in life. The launch pad for him and his wife to become successful entrepreneurs in their own right.

Paul's thoughts must have been overtaken by sleep, for he opened his eyes suddenly, sensing time had passed without him realising. It came into his head he'd been awoken by a sound.

But all was silent.

Then he heard voices coming from downstairs.

The surprise sent a shot of fear through him. Were there intruders in the house? Would he have to deal with them? Was it the tricksters who'd been terrifying his family?

Silence fell again. He turned on the bedside light, and as he started to look around the room for an implement to defend or attack, he heard a man's voice crying out.

"Put the knife down, for God's sake!"

It sounded like a struggle taking place. Things smashing on the floor, chairs scraping, falling over. It was followed by a woman's piercing scream.

Paul's blood ran cold as he grabbed a pair of scissors from the dressing table and flung open the bedroom door. Someone was being attacked downstairs.

Darkness and silence confronted him through the open door. He fumbled for the landing light switch and turned it on. Cautiously he moved to the top of the landing stairway, listening, looking with hawk eyes.

It was dark and silent downstairs. The landing light cast his elongated shadow eerily down the stairwell. Paul was fighting hard to suppress his growing feeling of terror. Slowly he descended the stairs, every creak amplified, every glance magnified.

At the bottom he switched on the hall light. Confidence slowly returned. The front door was locked. He checked around the house. No-one else was present, but as he assured himself he was entirely alone and safe in the house, the puzzle of what he'd heard remained.

He began to convince himself that the fears of his family had had a more profound effect on his mind, his subconscious, than he'd realised. Comforting himself with the thought, he entered the kitchen to make a relaxing cup of tea before returning to bed.

He crossed the room to fill the kettle. Then he noticed the carving knife laid on the counter beside the knife-block. He stopped, staring at it for a moment. It just lay there, totally harmless, inanimate. But strangely it seemed to convey some message of menace.

No, Paul wasn't going to spook himself with all that nonsense. His wife must have forgotten to put it back in the block and obviously, he reasoned, he hadn't noticed it laying there until now. He picked the knife up and replaced it in its rightful holder. Ghosts, supernatural, just a load of phooey he told himself.

Next morning Paul tried hard to concentrate on his work, an architectural design for a new office block. But his mind kept wandering back to the previous night.

He was trying to convince himself he'd heard the voices in a dream, and had awoken with his thoughts still residing in the subconscious for a while. However, he couldn't quite rest with that reasoning. And the knife on the counter? His wife must have left it there.

Try as he did, he was unable to settle with these explanations. It seemed silly, but perhaps his wife was right. Perhaps some sort of energy was released when something dreadful had happened. If someone had died horribly.

It was all nonsense of course, but he decided he should try and discover if any gruesome event had taken place in the house. At least if he could prove it hadn't, that would dispel the theory of after-life visitations upsetting his family.

The man who'd sold the house to him, Edwin Hurst, had said he was moving to a village about twenty miles away. Maybe he could help with its history.

Paul opened the bottom drawer of his desk and pulled out a bundle of papers and documents relating to the house purchase. The seller had left him a forwarding address for mail. He was sure there was a phone number there too. However, a search for the number proved fruitless.

Edwin Hurst's house wasn't that far away. The village was called Fulton. Paul could be there within the hour. He'd drive over that evening when the man was more likely to be at home.

Paul settled to his work in a better frame of mind, now that he'd resolved a plan of action.

Before leaving for Hurst's home, Paul rang his wife and spoke to the children. Diane asked if he'd arranged to put the house on the market. She was annoyed her husband had taken no action on this front.

"We need to get moving and look for somewhere else to live. We can't keep the children out of school for long," she urged.

Paul agreed, but he was hoping he could solve the problem that had beset them. He really didn't want to move unless absolutely necessary.

"I'll see the agent tomorrow." It was a promise that might take a little longer than his words of intention.

The rain was pouring down in the darkness as Paul arrived in his car outside Mr Hurst's house. In the dimness

17

of a street light, he could see it was set amid a row of old, brick-built cottages with small front gardens. He grabbed his umbrella off the back seat, made his way to the front door and rang the bell.

An unfriendly stare under a straggle of dark, wavy hair hair confronted him as the door opened. Dressed in a green T-shirt and blue jeans, the man's stocky, muscular body was silhouetted in the hall light.

"Mr Hurst?" Paul had met him a couple of times during the house sale transaction, but on those occasions the man had been smartly dressed. He looked different now.

He grunted confirmation, looking quizzical.

Paul identified himself and asked if he could have a chat. Edwin Hurst stared a little longer then remembered the man who had bought his former home.

He invited Paul into the living room, a sparse setting with a sofa and TV. The walls and ceiling were deeply browned, crying for redecoration. The man had obviously sold the much better house he'd lived in for a lesser property. Perhaps he'd needed to release some capital.

He indicated the sofa for Paul to sit down. But seeing the stains and ingrained dirt on its surface, Paul politely declined.

"If it's the damp patch on the wall you've come about, your surveyor should have told you about that. I can't be held responsible now." Hurst was on the defensive.

"No, it's nothing to do with any damp patches," Paul assured him.

He explained the reason for his visit. The strange events that had unsettled his family. Apparitions of an old couple in the house.

"I was wondering if you knew of anything..." he searched for the words, "... that might have happened there? Anything that might cause it to be haunted?"

Paul felt silly. He was anticipating his question to be met by peals of laughter. The ludicrous idea of paranormal activity.

But Hurst's expression was troubled, as if it could be a serious consideration. His eyes seemed to be recalling a distant event in the back of his mind. The moment quickly passed.

"No. Never had any problems like that," he dismissed the possibility.

As he spoke, Paul caught sight of a framed photograph perched on an occasional table. It displayed a man and woman, probably in their sixties, smiling with their arms around each others' shoulders. The man had a vivid red birthmark on his left cheek. Paul was shocked.

His daughter Rosemary had described the elderly man in the supposed apparition she'd seen as bearing a red birthmark on his left cheek.

Containing his surprise, Paul decided to redirect the conversation by asking about the photograph.

Hurst looked puzzled for a moment, but felt there was no harm in it.

"Those are my parents," he crossed to the table and picked up the photograph.

"Victor, or Vic as he's called, and Sylvia."

Paul took a closer look. The man in the photo definitely had a large, red birthmark on his cheek.

"They're retired now," Paul's host continued, replacing the frame on the table.

"They used to live in the house you bought from me, but decided to spend their twilight years living near the sea," Hurst recounted.

"So I took over the house and they moved to a caravan park at Windhaven on the east coast. They love it there," he explained.

Paul's visit left him with more questions than answers. Somehow he wasn't convinced by Edwin Hurst. And he was unsettled by seeing the man's father in the photograph. The birthmark appeared to fit his daughter's description of her ethereal visitor.

That night Paul slept restlessly, having strange dreams of shadowy figures following him and being trapped in a dark room. Beyond that, nothing out of the ordinary happened until he went downstairs in the morning to eat breakfast.

Resting on the counter in the kitchen was the carving knife. This time the sight of it shook him. He was absolutely certain he hadn't removed it from the block. Either someone was able to sneak into the house to play this strange prank unnoticed, or there really was an unearthly presence at work.

But whichever cause – why? Paul tended to think there was a rational explanation, though this belief was gradually eroding.

Whatever it was, for the moment he had to crack on with with his business. It was beginning to suffer from the events. But he resolved that at lunchtime he'd visit the local police station to see if there may have been any past troubles, or unusual happenings on record about the house.

Paul drove to the police station, situated in a busy high street, a couple of miles from his home. The officer at the reception desk was studying some documents as he approached.

"Can I help you, sir?" the policeman turned his gaze on the newcomer.

Paul hesitated for a moment. He wasn't quite sure how to pose the problem.

"I've recently moved into a house in the area, and there seems to be some strange activity going on there," he began.

"Strange activity?" the officer queried in a tone heavy with scepticism. "How so?"

Paul explained where he lived and the troubling events, beginning to wonder from the policeman's doubtful expression if he was sounding like a nutcase.

"So you're wondering if people were attacked there, possibly murdered, and now their ghosts are haunting the place?"

Put like that, Paul realised it came over as someone who might not be entirely of this planet. But it was an assumption that might be worth looking into. Except he personally hadn't seen any ghosts. And he wasn't himself entirely convinced.

"I'm not sure we can help you," the officer was masking his inner thoughts with a wall of politeness. But just in case he might be missing a vital point, he decided to call a superior, Detective Inspector, George Bird, a no-nonsense policeman.

Paul was invited to wait in an interview room. A few minutes later, Inspector Bird entered, a grey-haired man in his middle years, with a face burdened by weary experience.

Once again, Paul recounted what had happened.

"So you've seen a photograph in this man's house, what was his name?" asked the inspector.

"Edwin Hurst."

"Yes, Edwin Hurst. And the person in the photo had a birthmark on his face like the apparition your daughter saw?" The inspector paused. He sat opposite Paul in the interview room, resting his elbows on the table between them, stroking his chin in thought.

"Well that isn't exactly evidence of anything," the officer concluded. "I could hardly launch an investigation based on ghosts."

"But I just wanted to know if there were police records of any criminal activities, perhaps a murder at the house in the past," Paul realised the conversation was going nowhere. He felt a fool. But he was desperate to find a solution and get his family life back on track.

"Well, I'll check the records for you," Inspector Bird didn't actually think his visitor was round the bend, just deeply troubled by family problems unrelated to any macabre events. He wasn't planning to make serious enquiries on what he'd heard. He'd be laughed out of the police station.

"You look as though you're under a lot of stress. I suffer that too," the police officer sympathised. "Go along to your doctor, and ask him to give you something to steady your nerves. And get in some long walks. You'll feel better then."

The inspector's advice was well intentioned, but came over as patronising.

Paul decided he would make some further enquiries of his own.

In the evening he called his wife, but didn't mention his visit to the police station. She asked if he'd put the house on the market.

"I'm going to find out what's behind the strange events here," he replied. "I don't want to sell-up just like that."

"The children need to be settled," Diane was becoming angry. "If you won't do it, I will. But I wanted us to be in agreement."

"Give me a few days," Paul reasoned. "If I can't get to the bottom of it by then, I'll instruct the estate agent. I promise."

Diane reluctantly agreed the terms, though she doubted the family could ever be happy in the house again.

The following day Paul prepared for his next plan of action. He called his clients to say an elderly relative was unwell and not expected to live long. He'd be unavailable until tomorrow. His intention was to drive to the residential caravan park in Windhaven, near the east coast town of Great Yarmouth in Norfolk.

Edwin Hurst said his parents now lived there in retirement. He had no idea which particular caravan home they resided in, but he'd ask around. Perhaps, when he found them, they could shed some light on any strange history attached to the house.

It even crossed his mind that maybe they still had some access to the house and that's who his wife and daughters had seen. Though, on balance, it was ludicrous to think that the elderly couple would be wandering around the property, especially in the middle of the night. He quickly dismissed the possibility. Events were beginning to affect his imagination, he feared.

As Paul left the house, he saw a man in a smart, dark suit standing on the pavement by his front driveway.

"Hello, I'm Alan Spencer from across the road. Hope you're settling in okay."

Paul approached and shook the man's hand, saying everything was fine.

"Glad to see a normal family living here," said his neighbour. "The last lot were very reclusive, especially their son. Unfriendly."

His words set Paul thinking.

"Did anything unusual ever happen here?" he asked.

His neighbour looked puzzled.

"Nothing I know about," he replied. "Except the old boy and girl seemed to disappear some time ago. Their son said

25

they'd retired to some place on the east coast. Never liked him. Shifty type."

Paul wanted to press him for more information.

"Anyway, I've got to get to work," the neighbour began to walk away. "Nice talking to you. Catch up another time."

It took several hours of driving then searching down country lanes before Paul saw a sign to Windhaven Residential Caravan Park. The sat-nav was off target by a few miles.

The static homes were all neatly lined in rows on a slight incline, with cliff top views across the sea. It would be pot luck choosing the caravan he wanted, or of anyone knowing the couple he sought.

He knocked on several doors enquiring. None of the people he asked had ever heard of a Mr and Mrs Vic and Sylvia Hurst living there.

Paul was beginning to think his search would be in vain.

He tried a few more homes and was ready to give up, when an elderly man answering his call raised some hope.

"Never heard of them myself," he said, standing at the door in rolled up shirt sleeves, clasping a mug of tea with hands covered in soil from gardening. "But my wife knows everyone round here."

"Gladys," he turned and called her.

A few moments later Gladys appeared at the door, cradling a ginger cat in her arms. The woman's inquisitive gaze was framed by long, silvery hair that had long ago forsaken youthful colours.

Her husband explained why Paul had called. She thought for a moment, softly stroking the cat.

"Oh, Vic and Sylvia," she remembered. "They lived over that way," she raised her arm to point the direction and the cat leapt to the ground. It turned to Paul and starting to sniff at his trouser leg. He stepped back.

"Vic and Sylvia Hurst," Gladys was searching her mind. "Their caravan was called Rosamund. I don't think they're living there now though. It's owned by Mr Wilson. Give him a call. Nice chap. He might be able to tell you where they've gone."

Paul thanked the couple and made his way across to Mr Wilson's caravan.

A very old gentleman answered his call. He was stooped, looked frail and had difficulty hearing. After a long conversation, in which Paul struggled to make himself understood, the man could only partly help.

"I never met Mr and Mrs Hurst," Mr Wilson explained in a hoarse voice, clutching the door frame for support. "Their son handled the sale. They weren't living here when I viewed the place. It was empty." He paused for breath.

"Their son said they'd moved in with him. I think his name is Edwin, maybe Edward. Something like that. No idea where he lives though."

The man looked exhausted and Paul was obviously not going to learn any more. He thanked him and left.

Back in his car and driving home, Paul's thoughts were even more troubled. Edwin Hurst had told him his parents were living at the caravan park. But the old man, living in what was supposedly their home, had said they were living with their son.

Someone was lying, and it didn't appear to be the elderly gentleman. A dreadful thought struck Paul. Had Edwin Hurst disposed of his parents?

It seemed ludicrous. Why would a son murder his own parents?

Paul tried to dismiss the thought. You read about that sort of thing in newspapers. The chances of coming across it are remote. And yet the possibility wouldn't leave his mind. The 'ghosts' his wife and children had seen. The red birthmark Rosemary had described. It matched the birthmark on the face of Hurst's father in the photo. No. It was ridiculous. Or was it?

Paul rang his wife again that evening. This time he told Diane he'd tried to track Hurst's parents, but had drawn a blank. That he suspected the possibility of foul play.

"You're not a fucking detective!" Diane exploded. "You've got children. They're missing their education. We need to live. If you lose your work before I can find some, we'll have more to worry about than whether someone's been bumped off!"

"I'm trying to find a way of staying in our house. The one we built so many plans around," Paul pleaded.

"I never want to go back there," his wife yelled. "If you don't put the place up for sale tomorrow, I'll do it!" She hung up.

Paul was deeply upset, though he understood his wife's feelings. She was right. He was becoming obsessed with his suspicions. His family must come first. But...

He sat on the sofa in the living room lost in thought. After a while, he resolved to pay a visit on inspector George Bird one more time. Surely, if the detective knew the conflicting accounts of where Hurst's parents were supposedly living, he'd become interested in pursuing the case.

The inspector wore a resigned expression as he listened to Paul in the interview room. How many people in his long career had recounted their suspicions of possible grisly crimes to him, and when investigated had turned out to be fantasy or mischief making? He'd lost count.

"Well, it's quite possible, probable even, that this Hurst fellow has fallen out with his parents and just told the man who bought their caravan home that they're living with him," the inspector explained to Paul.

"People tell little white lies all the time to save themselves embarrassment." The officer was tiring of having to deal with someone who apparently had ghost troubles. Hardly a pretext for investigation by the police.

Paul realised he was getting nowhere. He had no evidence that anything criminal had happened. He conceded it was time to move on for the sake of his family. But nagging doubts remained.

CHAPTER 2

EDWIN HURST was unsettled by Paul's visit. He wondered if the man who'd bought his house knew more than he was giving away.

What disturbed him most was the revelation that Paul's family may have seen his parents in the house. But that was impossible. They were dead. He'd killed them when they'd come to see him on a visit from their caravan home at Windhaven.

Ghosts didn't really exist, he knew that. And yet?

He began to doubt if he had killed them. That somehow they'd survived. But no, that wasn't possible. He'd stabbed them repeatedly with the carving knife in the kitchen.

Then he waited until dark to load the bodies into his van, rolling them up separately in large rugs. The five mile journey to the quarry, where he worked at the time, seemed an eternity. Any second he feared he might be stopped by the police. But it passed without incident.

The next difficult part was distracting Wayne Vernon, the other duty operative at the works. He could see his colleague in the light of the cabin control room, perched high above the quarry rock crushing machinery.

Hurst knew his mobile phone number and rang it, having taken the precaution of using a different SIM card in his own phone, so his operative wouldn't recognise the incoming caller.

Putting on a false voice he said: "Mr Vernon, this is Woodbridge police station calling. There's been an accident and your wife is in St Mary's General Hospital. You must come quickly."

"What's happened?" cried the distraught operative, believing the wicked lie.

"Just come quickly," Hurst commanded in his fake tone.

He could see his workmate in the control room rushing to the door. Within seconds he was frantically descending the exterior metal stairway from the cabin.

"I've got to go!" Wayne shouted to Hurst as he reached the bottom.

"Something's happened."

In a moment he was in his car and racing away.

Hurst knew he should phone his boss to report the operative's absence. One person working alone at the plant would breach safety regulations. But it could wait.

He lifted the bodies of his parents, rolled-up in the rugs, from the back of the van. He was a strong man, but struggled under their weight as he carried them in turn on his shoulder up the metal stairway to the plant landing.

Then he hauled them towards the quarry's primary crusher, enclosed by a wire safety cage.

Unbolting the cage door, he unrolled his mother and father from the rugs and pulled them on to the platform inside.

Their eyes stared vacantly upwards, their clothes steeped in dried blood stains. He released his grip on their hands and walked back the short distance to the control room, where he activated the quarry crusher.

A deafening roar broke out as huge, rotating steel blades inside a metal chute sprang viciously into life. Giant boulders of limestone rock began to descend from a conveyor belt and plunged into the chute. Within seconds they were smashed apart by the mighty force of the blades.

The rock then descended into a secondary crusher, pulverising the rock into yet smaller pieces, and onwards to yet another crusher until the once proud boulders were spat out into a growing pile of mere stones.

From here, they would be scooped into a truck in the morning and used to make tarmac for road surfaces, or concrete for construction.

Hurst returned to the primary crusher platform, and in turn hoisted his deceased mother and father into the chute. Blood spurted as the blades set to work. In moments their minced bodies were on a violent journey to oblivion.

Their son hosed down the bloodstains in the chute. Any small traces that were left soon became covered in fragments of limestone grit and dust as more stone boulders cascaded into the jaws of the crusher.

He bagged up the rug shrouds in heavy duty, black plastic sacks and threw them on the site skip. By mid-morning tomorrow, they'd be buried under a ton of quarry rubble. Finally, he phoned his boss to report that his fellow operative had been urgently called away.

Hurst lost his job at the quarry a short time later due to his uncontrollable temper. One day the boss told him his work performance was below par - so he punched him in the face.

Two years had passed since those events, and things had been going well.

But now, the man who had bought his house, Paul Hunter, seemed to be prying into his life. And why had the family seen an old couple in his former home? Apparitions as had been described to him.

Had the new owner discovered something that linked him to the murder of his parents? Had the man found some clue that was overlooked when he was disposing of them? Was he trying to trick him into a give-away confession? Most of all. Did he need to do something about Paul Hunter and his family?

As Hurst drove to his former house, his mind was searching for a plan of action should it become necessary to dispose of Mr Hunter. It was evening in late October. He'd decided to call at this time of day estimating his possible target would probably be back from work. He was unaware that Paul mostly worked from home.

Lights illuminated the drawn window curtains as Hurst pulled up outside the property.

Paul was surprised to see the person he suspected of hiding a dark secret standing at his front door. The visitor was smiling and smartly dressed, in contrast to their last meeting. Paul didn't want him in his house, but it was not his nature to be offensive.

"I was in the area, so I thought I'd call," Hurst began. "I think I was probably a bit short with you when you came the other night. I just wanted to apologise."

Paul invited him in. Hurst knew the layout of his former home by heart, but he wanted to see how the living area had been re-arranged, in case he needed to break-in at a later stage. Paul offered his visitor a cup of coffee, which was accepted.

"I've had a lot on my mind recently and been a bit bad tempered with everyone," Hurst continued with his phoney excuse for the visit.

Paul dismissed it. Not a problem. He understood.

"It concerned me that you've had some strange experiences here," Hurst was now as falsely friendly and sociable as his personality could struggle to achieve.

Paul admitted the odd events besetting his family were puzzling and had put considerable strain on them all.

Hurst believed he was doing a great job of fooling Paul into thinking he was a perfectly good person, unaware that his host knew of the lie about his parents still living at the caravan park.

But no matter how much Hurst thought he was making a good impression on Paul, his fake outward persona could not hide his intrinsic, unpleasant nature. His eyes betrayed a devious, shifty inner soul. Paul considered Hurst was unstable and it would be best to keep him calm, and give no clue that he'd been enquiring about his parents.

After making the coffee, Paul sat with his visitor at the dining table. It was situated at the far end of the living room, awaiting a permanent location when redecoration was completed. Hurst could see a computer and filing cabinets through the open door of the adjoining room.

"Do you work from home?" he enquired.

"Mostly," Paul replied. He felt uncomfortable. He didn't want to tell this man anything about how he lived. He wanted him to leave as soon as possible without appearing to be rude.

"Nothing strange ever happened when I lived here," Hurst continued the conversation. "Did your wife and children say what the old couple they saw looked like?"

Paul began to suspect his visitor was on a fishing trip. Why would he be concerned about his family, or what they'd seen? It was not his house anymore.

"They said the old man had a large, red birthmark on his left cheek," Paul told him.

Hurst's jaw dropped. Once again he began to wonder if somehow his parents had survived the quarry rock crusher. But that was impossible. He had witnessed their bodies being pulverised by the huge metal blades. No, ghosts do not exist. Something funny was going on. Was this man Paul Hunter trying to set a trap for him?

Paul had seen Hurst's amazed reaction, and it confirmed to him there was definitely something wrong. He knew not what. He didn't believe in ghosts either. But something very strange was happening.

His visitor's countenance had rapidly changed from overtly friendly to troubled. He was certain he'd got away with the murder of his parents. Was this man going to be his nemesis?

"Well I hope you sort out the problem," Hurst rose from the chair. "I'd better not keep you any longer. As I say, sorry I seemed a bit rude the other night."

Hurst walked down the hall towards the front door, then veered off through an open doorway into the kitchen.

"I'd always had it in mind to replace all these units with modern stuff," Hurst spouted his excuse for diverting into the room, gazing at the tired and faded cupboards.

As he spoke, he eyed the knife-block on the counter. It would be easy to reach for the carving blade and carry out the execution in seconds. But he wouldn't have time to clean-up. And he had no plan for efficient disposal of the body. Paul's family would probably arrive before he could finish. And then he would have to....it would be messy.

"We were planning to replace all these old units soon," Paul took up the topic, unaware his visitor was considering options for killing him.

"I expect your wife is out right now, looking at what she wants fitted," Hurst surmised.

"She's been so terrified by this place, she's moved with the kids to her parents at Bridgeworth." As he uttered the words, Paul realised he shouldn't have said anything. He deeply distrusted this man.

Hurst smiled. Now he knew Paul's family were elsewhere. Even better, where they were living. If necessary, he could find their exact location in Bridgeworth. A plan was forming in his mind.

"Well, it was good to meet you again," Hurst oozed falsely, as he stood by the front door preparing to leave.

Paul nodded. He couldn't bring himself to respond with any greater affirmative and began to close the door.

"Oh," Hurst shook his head as if he'd forgotten to mention something. "Take my phone number, in case you want to contact me again."

Paul didn't want his number, but thought it easier to accept and send the man on his way as quickly as possible. He jotted it on a piece of paper then bade his visitor farewell, closing the door with a growing sense of unease.

Hurst walked to his car. He suspected Paul Hunter was harbouring some information on his dark past. Beneath the innocent exterior Hurst portrayed, he was feeling stressed. He needed to get away for a while. To relax. To plan.

There was a pleasant hotel at the seaside resort of Calbourne on the south coast, where in happy, earlier times he spent holidays with his parents. They were fond memories. He wanted them back again. It was a pity everything since had turned sour.

Hurst started to drive home. After a few minutes the phone call he was expecting came through.

"You've left some keys here," Paul informed him.

"Have I?" Hurst replied. He paused. "So I have. My house keys. Lucky I left my number with you. I'll pop back."

Hurst smiled. While Paul had been making the coffee, he'd deliberately placed a set of keys on the carpet beneath his chair at the dining table. Then he'd obscured the view of them with his legs while they'd been talking.

Paul would have found them at some point and rung him. The call came sooner rather than later. Hurst had a duplicate set of keys anyway. But now he also had Paul's phone number logged on his mobile, without raising the slightest hint of suspicion by asking for it. That could prove very useful in the future.

Paul was thrilled to see his children at the weekend. But in the evening, after the pleasantries with Rosemary, Alice and his wife's parents, it was time for a serious private conversation with Diane. She was frosty. Paul still hadn't put the house on the market.

He described in detail how he'd spent his time checking out Hurst, The visit to the caravan park where his parents supposedly lived, and his thoughts of suspecting foul play.

"You're not a bloody private detective," she once again angrily reminded him. "Stop wasting your time investigating and possibly losing clients. The children's education is suffering. We need to settle them in a new home. They will never be happy in that place."

"I know, I know," Paul agreed. "But if there's been a murder, we have a duty to..." he struggled for the words, "...to bring it to light."

"That's the police's job. Not yours," Diane was becoming extremely heated.

"But they don't believe anything has happened," Paul explained.

"Well they're hardly going to launch a major investigation on what you think. Not without evidence," his wife was losing patience.

"He called round the other night."

"Who?" Diane was puzzled.

"Edwin Hurst, the man we bought the house from."

Diane was silent for a moment, thinking.

"Why? Does he suspect you've been making enquiries about him?" She seemed worried.

"No. He just wanted to pop in for a social visit. To say sorry he'd been a bit rude when I'd called on him to ask if anything unusual had happened at the house."

"So the man you suspect of murder is now paying social visits. For Christ's sake, leave it alone," Diane insisted.

"Okay," Paul was resigned to protecting the interests of his family.

"We will seriously have to think about our future together if you don't start selling that bloody, cursed house now," his wife fired a warning shot. She'd had enough. "If you don't, I'll find accommodation locally, and arrange for the kids to go to school in this area. I can't live with my parents here forever."

It dawned on Paul that he would not be spending a peaceful weekend with his wife and children as things currently stood. The friction would only upset the girls. Next morning he left after breakfast, telling his daughters he had an urgent business meeting.

Back at home he felt tired and miserable. He unpacked clothes from his overnight bag and showered to freshen up. Then he went to the kitchen to make a coffee.

As he entered, he saw the carving knife laying on the counter next to the knife-block. He knew that he definitely hadn't removed it.

A bizarre scenario suddenly flashed into his mind. Had Hurst come into house while Paul was away? The door locks hadn't been changed since he'd moved in. The keys had been handed over at purchase, but Hurst could have kept duplicates.

Had the man contrived some plan with his parents to terrorise Paul's family? To give the impression the place was haunted? Letting themselves in to play tricks? But why?

Perhaps if they succeeded, they could buy back the house at a knock-down price because Paul would be only to happy to re-sell.

No. The idea was ludicrous. He feared he was starting to crack-up with the strain. But something was not right. His next priority was to change the locks. That would make him feel a little more secure.

Paul had just finished arranging a valuation visit from the local estate agent when the doorbell rang. He descended the stairs from his office to answer the call.

Standing in the doorway was Detective Inspector, George Bird. It took Paul by surprise. The officer was the last person he expected to see again after he'd dismissed his concerns about Hurst.

"May we talk?" the Inspector's request conveyed an air of mystery. He was wearing a dark overcoat and trilby hat which he removed as he entered the house. Paul took him into the living room and invited him to sit on the sofa.

"No thanks. I can't stay long." Inspector Bird was looking round the room with searching eyes as he spoke, taking in the detail of the layout. Then his attention turned to Paul.

"After our conversation the other day," he began, "I decided to make a few enquiries about Edwin Hurst, the man who sold you this house."

Paul listened with interest as the inspector continued.

"It appears he has three criminal convictions for violent assault on people and has served a prison sentence for fraud."

Paul stared in amazement.

"I knew there was something wrong," he uttered.

"It also seems his parents' pensions are being paid into his own bank account," the detective revealed. He paused for a moment.

"Now there's nothing necessarily unusual about that. Sons and daughters will sometimes have their elderly parents' pensions paid into their accounts. It saves them from having to cope with new technologies they don't understand."

"But his parents don't live where he says they live," Paul interrupted.

The detective gave him a withering look. He was not taking comments at this stage.

"I know, and I've made enquiries about that too, if you will allow me to finish. That is why I have decided to widen my investigation. There may have been fraudulent activity."

"And if his parents are...?" Paul didn't finish the dreadful supposition. "Could it be those spectres my wife and children saw of an elderly man and woman really are...?"

The inspector shook his head.

"Ghosts are not in my remit. Tangible evidence is what I look for. Spectres do not testify in court. One step at a time please."

"I understand," Paul replied. "It's just that this whole business has torn my family apart."

The detective showed no sign of sympathy. It was not his role to become emotionally involved.

"I came here primarily to warn you about Hurst," the officer continued, "given his tendency to violence. And to ask if you know anything else about him beyond what you've already told me."

Paul recounted Hurst's visit, which had seemed a bit strange to him. But there was nothing more he could add.

"Oh, I've got his phone number if you want it," Paul remembered.

"We've already got that," Inspector Bird replied.

"Are you going to question him?"

"Well, we'd like to, but he appears to be missing," the officer put on his hat, preparing to leave. "We're making enquiries."

He walked to the front door. Just before departing he gave Paul a serious warning.

"In the meantime, make sure you lock up well at night. If Hurst contacts you again, let me know straight-away." The inspector handed him a contact card.

CHAPTER 3

EDWIN HURST strolled along the edge of the sandy beach at Calbourne, the waves lapping gently on the shore.

It was late in the year, but he remembered the warm, sunny days when he was a boy on holiday with his mum and dad. They helped him build sandcastles and splashed around with him in the sea. They were happy days. Good days.

But the world had become less friendly as he grew up. It didn't understand him. Or he didn't understand it. So he pulled a few tricks. Who didn't? You had to survive.

Once he'd nearly married. But she was becoming oppressive. Making too many rigid plans for their life together. Then she discovered he spent some of his nights in the company of woman who sold themselves.

What was wrong with it? They weren't vying for his affections. It was a transaction, pure...well not so much pure, but simple. No strings. That's how he justified it.

Just as well he and his betrothed parted when they did, thought Hurst. He may well have ended up parting from her in a more final way if they'd actually become hitched. He found it difficult to cope with people who disagreed with him.

His legs were beginning to feel tired with the walk along the beach. He crossed the sand towards the sea wall fronting the quarter mile stretch of the small, curved bay. Climbing the stone steps up to the promenade, he made his way to an empty wooden bench. He sat down to enjoy the peace and watch the rippling waves.

In the summer, the place would be teeming with people. There were still some late-season holidaymakers, taking advantage of the cheap accommodation prices, but there was now room everywhere to relax, despite the slight chill in the air.

As Hurst rested back on the bench absorbing the atmosphere, he became aware of two people sitting on either side of him. He hadn't noticed them approach or sit down.

Suddenly he heard a voice on his left.

"I always said to your mother, no good would come of you."

Hurst turned his head in the direction. His elderly father was sitting beside him, his eyes narrowing as he spoke, distorting the aged lines of his face into a hideous, glaring mask.

Another voice came from Hurst's right.

"I always defended you when your father said that Edwin. But he was right!"

Hurst turned to see his mother sitting beside him, wearing her favourite, floral cotton dress. Her plump, round face was cast in regret and disappointment.

"You've just been a waster and liar, all down the line. And for all the help we gave you, you killed us!" Hurst's father rounded on him.

"That was wicked, evil!" His mother scolded, pointing her finger at him.

"Nothing but criticism, that's all I ever got from you," Hurst shouted back at his parents. He stood up to confront them.

"I could never do right!" He was incensed and broke into a barrage of insults about his mother and father's shortcomings.

Passers-by stared, amazed and fearful of this strange man's behaviour. He seemed to be aiming his vitriolic attack at an empty bench.

As Hurst's fury rose to a crescendo, he looked again and saw the bench was unoccupied. The reality of his surroundings gradually came to him. His parents weren't there. He swore at the onlookers. They pretended not to notice and hurried on their way.

His mind was in turmoil. He must have imagined seeing his mother and father. They were dead. He knew. But their criticisms of him, real or imagined, cut like a barb. Yes he'd been a failure, but they didn't need to rub it in.

The import business he'd set up, with money borrowed from them, had failed because the cheap computers he hoped would undercut the big boys were sub-standard. The complaints mounted and drove him into liquidation.

His parents lent him yet more money to start up a cafe. But his less than sociable reaction if a customer ever complained, led to a loss of reputation and essential custom.

With large losses, he engineered a fire on the premises in the hope the insurance payout would cover the deficit. But investigators discovered large quantities of flammable liquid, that is petrol, had been spread around the premises, which had considerably aided the conflagration. For that criminal act, Hurst was sentenced to three years in prison.

Yes, he'd fucked up, but they were his parents. They had no right to condemn him as a failure.

Anyway, he pulled a master stroke in the end.

In order for him to avoid paying death duty taxes on the house when they died, he persuaded his parents to sign over ownership of the property into his name. They'd be assured of a home until they passed away, and the family wouldn't be losing any money to the government.

It was a great idea and duly executed – not long afterwards he executed them. He was smiling again, with a valuable asset in property.

Of course, Hurst also pulled another smart move. To save his parents the hassle of adapting to 21st-century technology, he organised for them to have their pensions paid into his account. In this way, he could withdraw the money and give it to them in hard cash, which they much preferred.

Since they had never officially died, the income now streamed entirely to him.

Everything had been ticking like clockwork, until that bastard Paul Hunter, who'd bought his home, came into his life. Hurst was growing more and more convinced that the man knew something about his past, that he'd discovered his murky secret. And now he would probably have to seek revenge, even to silence him.

He had no idea, of course, that Paul knew nothing about him, other than the feeling the man was unpleasant and the information the police inspector had imparted to him.

Hurst made his way back to the hotel where he was staying, walking down a side street from the beach front. As he approached the premises, he saw a police car parked outside. Two officers were studying his car, parked on the roadside nearby.

Hurst turned away and started to walk in the opposite direction.

What did they know? Has Hunter told them something? He was beginning to panic. *Keep calm, keep calm.* He fought to reassure himself.

He walked down several side streets, wondering why the police were looking at his car, struggling to think of what to do next. After a while, he cautiously approached the hotel again. The police car had gone.

Hurst climbed the short flight of steps to the hotel entrance, afraid a hiding police officer might pounce on him. Inside, as he crossed the lobby to the lift that would take him to his room, the desk clerk called to him.

"Mr Hurst."

He stopped.

"Can I have a word."

Hurst approached the desk.

The young man explained that two policemen had called, looking for him. They didn't say what it was about. They left a card asking him to call them as soon as he returned to the hotel.

Hurst took the card.

"Oh, it's probably about my parking ticket. I forgot to return the form," he lied. "I'll call them."

The clerk gave a sympathetic smile.

Hurst returned to his room. He'd decided it was time to leave. His mind was racing. *They must have traced me by the car number plate. They don't do that for trivial matters.*

They obviously haven't got anything solid, or else they'd be swarming the place. But they probably want to ask some serious questions. Time to disappear.

He was annoyed that his holiday was to be cut short. He'd only been away for a couple of days. After packing his bag, he returned to reception to pay the bill. If he left without paying, which he'd thought about, the hotel would call the police and set-off the alarm. He needed to quietly slip away.

He made the three hour drive back to his home, parking in a street around the corner, and walked the last part to his house to ensure there were no police officers waiting outside.

The sky was growing dark, so it was easier to blend unrecognised with passers-by on the opposite side of the road. There was no sign of any police presence.

He crossed the road and entered the house. He needed to get far away. A bit of space. He believed that if he kept out of sight for long enough, the police would tire of trying to find him. That was his hope. The idea of being questioned by the law terrified him. If they discovered the dreadful thing he'd done...

He never wanted to spend time in prison ever again. It was unbearable.

Hurst had £10,000 in cash stashed away in the house. It would buy him time. If he used cards at cash machines, the police would trace his location. He didn't have a current passport, so he couldn't leave the country. Anyway, the police could trace his destination from an airport.

He re-packed his travel bag with immediate needs for his next journey. He had the Scottish Highlands in the far north of the country in mind. It offered remote, out of the way places. But if he booked any accommodation online, it could be easily traced. He had another plan.

A police patrol car pulled up outside Hurst's home. The officer on the passenger side was calling in to headquarters on the radio. He was put through to Detective Inspector George Bird.

"Sir, you asked us to contact you if we saw any activity at 12 Peyton Street. We believe there is someone in the house. Do you want us to take further action?"

"No," the inspector replied. "I'll be along in ten minutes. Drive round the corner so the occupant can't see you, and wait until I call you."

The inspector left his office and drove to Hurst's address. He rang the doorbell. Hurst became worried at the sound. He wasn't expecting any callers. Was it the police? He remained still. If he waited, whoever was calling might go away.

Inspector Bird anticipated the reaction. So many people he visited to interview pretended they weren't in. He opened the letterbox and called out.

"You're house is on fire, quick!"

In reflex, Hurst rushed to the door and flung it open. The inspector stood there in his dark overcoat, his eyes analysing the suspect from beneath his trilby hat.

"Evening, Mr Hurst. I'm Detective Inspector George Bird," he introduced himself. "Could I have a word, please?"

Hurst's immediate response was to try and slam the door shut. The inspector's arm shot out to stop it.

"Things will go easier for you if you let me in peaceably," the inspector insisted.

Hurst relented and allowed him in. They went to the living room, where the officer noticed a travel bag on the sofa.

"Off to somewhere nice?" he enquired.

"No, I've just come back from a short break," Hurst replied.

"Paid for with your parents' pension income, no doubt," the inspector was looking for a reaction. His words struck home. Hurst stuttered a reply.

"What do you mean?" He looked offended.

Inspector Bird said he knew their pensions were being paid into Hurst's bank account. But as far as his enquiries revealed, his parents were nowhere to be found on the planet.

"Could you tell me where they are?" he asked.

Hurst was in a tight spot. How could he bluff his way out of this one? If he told the officer they lived on the caravan park, enquiries would soon show they weren't there. He'd try a different tactic.

"They used to live at a caravan park in Windhaven, on the east coast. But they recently moved into a new retirement home," he lied in desperation. "I'll get the details if you hang on a minute."

Hurst left the room. The inspector wondered if he might be planning to disappear from the house. If he wasn't back in a minute, he'd call the patrol car. In the meantime he looked around the room, wondering if he might see anything of interest to investigate.

The officer's back was turned as Hurst returned with a baseball bat. He raised it and felled the inspector with a blow to the back of his head. He staggered forward and slumped unconscious on the floor.

Hurst searched through his pockets. Did he have any evidence on him that showed he'd murdered his parents? He found the officer's identity card and pocketed it, thinking it might come in useful.

Then he found a slip of paper with a name and phone number. It was Paul Hunter's, the person who had bought his house. It confirmed to Hurst the man was an interfering busybody who'd set everything in motion.

Hunter had contacted him with all that hoo-ha about seeing ghosts. But really he was trying to trap him. As Hurst's paranoia grew, he realised that was why he'd seen his mother and father on the bench at the seaside.

They hadn't really been there, it was just Paul Hunter's auto-suggestion that had conjured them up in his mind.

But none of that changed the fact Hurst was now in deep shit. He'd attacked a police officer. Prison loomed. He couldn't bear the thought. The inspector would awake to tell all. He had to be permanently silenced.

Hurst rolled the inspector on to his back, then straddled his body and closed his hands around the victim's neck, gripping tightly.

The officer shuddered under the attack of being throttled. Even in unconsciousness, his body was struggling for survival. After a minute of fighting back, the inspector's eyes suddenly opened wide, staring with such venom that Hurst almost recoiled in terror. Then the policeman slumped, and was still.

The officers waiting in the police car around the corner radioed the inspector. They'd received an urgent message to attend a robbery at a corner shop half-a-mile away. There was no reply. They couldn't wait, the robbery suspect was escaping. The patrol car accelerated away to the hunt.

Hurst found a large section of plastic sheeting in his back-garden shed and carried it into the house. He laid it out on the living room floor. Then gathering up the inspector's trilby hat, he placed it back on the dead officer's head and rolled the body up in the plastic sheeting.

If the forensics people ever searched the house, he wanted to leave no evidence to prove something had happened to the inspector there.

The tricky bit now would be getting the body into the boot of his car without raising the suspicion of a passer-by in the street. Earlier he'd parked the vehicle around the corner, so he went to retrieve it, pulling up outside the house.

Returning to the garden shed, he hauled out a wheelbarrow. Hurst was a strong man, but he struggled to lift the dead weight of the inspector into it. When the body had been loaded, he wheeled the barrow to the car. As he opened the boot, a woman walking her dog on a lead down the street stopped beside him.

"Good Lord!" she began. "What have you got there? A dead body?"

Hurst felt panic rising. Would he have to dispose of her too? She smiled. He realised that in the reflection of the sodium street lighting, it was not easy to distinguish the content of the well wrapped plastic sheeting.

"Yes, it's my wife," he laughed, attempting to play it down with an albeit tasteless joke.

"I'm having a clear-out in the house," Hurst concocted a story. "I'll be taking this to the recycling depot tomorrow."

The woman smiled again. Her dog, an Alsatian, seemed to be taking an unwelcome interest at what was contained in the wheelbarrow. The animal was trying to climb up, sniffing excitedly at the plastic sheeting. The woman pulled at the lead. The dog reluctantly obeyed, moving on with its owner down the street.

Hurst couldn't tip the body into the boot, the bottom lip was too high. With extreme difficulty he had to hoist the lifeless inspector and drop him inside.

Returning to the house he collected his computer. The police weren't going to get hold of that and delve into what he had stored on it. He placed the equipment on the back seat floor.

Finally, he collected his travel bag, the baseball bat he'd used to club the officer and, from his garden shed, a pair of bolt cutters. Then he drove off.

Hurst headed for the quarry works, 15 miles away, where he had once been employed. He had no access to the rock crushers, having been summarily dismissed from the job two years earlier, but crushing was not his plan.

There was a narrow, dirt road to the side of the quarry leading to a small, deep-water lake. It was part of the old quarry operations, and had been formed by rock-blasting over the years, creating a chasm that was now filled with natural groundwater. The depth of the water was around 300 feet, and the lake was enclosed on all sides by a sheer rock precipice.

Deemed too dangerous for recreational purposes, a twenty foot high, wire-mesh security fence had been erected around the perimeter. That hadn't stopped foolhardy youths from testing their bravado on occasions, and drowning in the unforgiving waters.

Hurst drove in the darkness down the dirt track. The car's suspension rocked and baulked at the rutted, uneven surface that had been carved by the huge, quarry vehicles once plying its course.

When he'd worked at the quarry, the route was only used as an access to a remote area where spent equipment was stored, ready to be transferred to a scrap metal dealer.

At the end of the track, the car headlights picked out a metal gate. Now this was possibly the next tricky bit. In the time Hurst had left the quarry, he couldn't be sure of what changes may have taken place.

He knew the gate was padlocked, but he'd retained the key he'd been given to it during his employment. If, however, it had been changed, he had the bolt cutter with him. That too, he'd kept from his employer when he'd been sacked. It might come in handy one day, he thought. Never realising, until now, the dark purpose.

His fear was since his days there, a CCTV camera may have been erected. Or a security light. On the latter he was right. A floodlight shot into life as the car pulled up near the gate barrier. For a second he was blinded. As sight swiftly returned, he looked for posts, high points bordering the gate where cameras would be mounted. He could see none.

He climbed out of the car taking his travel bag and placed it on the ground. Then he approached the gate. Putting on a pair of gloves, he took the padlock key from his pocket.

The lock was rusted. The gate it appeared was now rarely used. Hurst inserted the key and tried to turn it. The mechanism resisted. He made several more attempts, but it refused to budge. The bolt cutter would be needed.

He removed the key, pulling it roughly. As he did so, the lock sprang open. It was so decayed, it had only been held in place by rust. The security light still worked, but the access had apparently been abandoned. Hurst considered this to be a good omen.

The gates juddered as he pulled them open. He returned to the car and released the handbrake. Then he went to the rear of the vehicle and, with a great effort, began to push it.

The track was on a slight uphill incline. It was hard work, but after several yards the slope dipped down.

The route curved to the right, but he pushed the car ahead on to the grass verge dividing the track and the lake. The downhill gradient increased and soon the vehicle began to move away from Hurst under its own momentum. It rocked on the uneven surface for a short distance, then suddenly disappeared from view, plunging 30 feet down the quarry face before violently impacting on the deep waters below.

Hurst heard the echoing smash as the vehicle hit the lake surface, followed by a softer, bubbling, gurgling as the car, computer, baseball bat and the unfortunate inspector, descended into the dark depths.

The view afforded by the security light extinguished as it timed out. Hurst stood there in the darkness, smiling for a moment. Then a cold feeling enveloped him. He had the strangest sensation someone was standing behind him.

He felt the hair on the back of his head begin to bristle. Slowly he turned, wondering who was watching him. In the darkness, he could only pick out vague shapes, but no-one else seemed to be there. For some reason, he had the oddest feeling the inspector had been present. But that was impossible. His body was now at the bottom of the lake.

Feeling slightly unnerved, he made his way back to the gate.

The security light came on again. Although it was a remote area, the illumination made him feel uncomfortable, as if shedding light for eyes to peer upon his evil act. He closed the gate and repositioned the padlock.

Collecting his travel bag, he reached inside and took out a torch. He'd need to avoid stumbling into deep ruts during his return journey on foot along the track.

As he carefully picked his way back toward the main road, he made a phone call.

"Hello Billy," Hurst greeted the man answering.

"Who's this?" came the reply.

"Remember me? Edwin Hurst?"

The man was silent for a moment.

"Edwin Hurst? From Pellridge?"

"The very same," Hurst replied.

They'd met when both had been serving time at Pellridge Prison in North Yorkshire. Hurst for arson and fraud; Billy Parsons for ringing cars, that is, giving stolen vehicles a new identity with forged documents and selling them on.

During their time in prison they'd become friends after realising their homes were not far from each other. Billy had promised Hurst that if ever he needed a favour, he'd be willing to help.

"I take it this is a business call?" Billy asked, having never heard from his former prison mate since their release.

"You could say," Hurst replied in a guarded tone.

"I run a legitimate car trade operation now," Billy informed him.

"I'm willing to pay," Hurst assured, "but I need a bit of help." He paused. "For old times' sake?"

Billy was silent for a moment before speaking.

"It'll cost you."

"I know," Hurst replied. "How much?"

"I could do it for £5,000."

Now Hurst was silent for a moment. That was half the money he possessed to sustain himself while he kept out of sight. Then he realised how he could solve the problem.

"Okay," he agreed.

Billy told him where his second-hand car trade business was situated. "It's all in my wife's name now – legitimate," he laughed. "My second wife that is. The first one left me when I was inside. She couldn't take it anymore."

Hurst sympathised, but really didn't give a damn if Billy's first wife had left him. Anyone who would marry an idiot like Billy must need their brains examining, he thought. But the man had his uses. Fortunately he still operated in the locality, ten miles away.

"See you here at eight tomorrow morning," Billy hung up.

In the meantime, Hurst couldn't return to his house with the likelihood of more police visits, so he'd have to bed down in the open until morning. He clambered behind some bushes lining the track and found a fairly even space in the long, damp grass.

He wore a thick, dark overcoat and trousers that helped to insulate him from the cold. The accommodation was uncomfortable, but he'd suffered worse. In a few hours he'd make for the main road and call a cab.

CHAPTER 4

PAUL HUNTER was asleep when he became aware of the front doorbell repeatedly ringing. It was accompanied by loud knocks on the door. He woke in a panic. The bedside clock displayed 3.30 in the morning.

He turned on the light and put on his dressing gown, wondering who the hell was calling at this time? What had happened?

Rushing down the stairs, he quickly unlocked the front door and opened it. A woman flanked by two uniformed police officers stood outside.

"I'm Detective Superintendent Susan Hopkin," she announced, raising an identity card in her right hand.

For a second Paul's blood ran cold, his legs faltered. *Christ! Had something happened to his family?*

D.S. Hopkin detected the fear in his face. "It's okay sir. It's nothing to upset yourself about. We're here to make some enquiries. Sorry to disturb you in the middle of the night. May we come in?"

Paul was deeply relieved the visit was nothing to do with bad news about his wife and children, but still perturbed by the sudden intrusion. It must be something important for them to call at this hour. He invited the officers inside.

If the detective hadn't identified herself as a police superintendent, Paul would have placed her as a businesswoman, fair-haired and smartly dressed in a dark-blue dress.

"I understand Detective Inspector George Bird came to see you a few days ago, making an enquiry about Edwin Hurst," D.S. Hopkin began.

Paul confirmed that he had.

"Has the inspector been in touch with you since?" she asked, closely studying Paul's reaction, which made him feel uncomfortable.

"No," he replied.

"Did he say where he might be going?"

Paul explained that the detective inspector had seemed suspicious of Hurst's activities, and warned him to be careful of any further contact with him.

"So you've no idea where the inspector might be?"

"None at all," Paul replied. "Why is there a problem?"

D.S. Hopkin didn't answer. She was not willing to reveal that the detective had apparently disappeared from the face of the earth. He hadn't reported back from his visit to Hurst, and a forced entry into the house revealed neither the owner or the officer being present.

And there was nothing that could give the detective superintendent a lead to their whereabouts. The missing computer, evidenced by a lonely monitor sitting on the desk, had heightened suspicions that all was not well. Repeated attempts to contact the inspector had proved fruitless.

Detective Hopkin seemed satisfied that Paul wasn't hiding anything.

She apologised for the abrupt intrusion. "If the inspector gets in touch with you, please let me know immediately," she gave him a card with contact details.

"Can you tell me what's happened?" It was obvious to Paul that the inspector was missing.

D.S. Hopkin decided some explanation was needed and confirmed that he had disappeared with no explanation.

"If Hurst contacts you, do not meet him. Let me know immediately." Beyond that the superintendent had no more to say for the time being.

Paul accompanied the officers to the front door. As he closed it, he began to realise he'd opened a can of worms by contacting Inspector Bird with his suspicions. Now it seemed he was missing. What had happened to him?

He entered the kitchen to make a cup of tea. He couldn't sleep for the moment.

For the second time that night his blood ran cold. The carving knife, which he definitely knew had been placed in the knife-block, was laying on the counter again. Something evil had happened in this house. Now he'd come around to his wife's way of thinking, and he believed it was something connected to Hurst.

The property was back on the market for sale. He felt guilty that he might be passing on these troubles to a new buyer, but his primary concern was the happiness and stability of his family.

Paul picked up the knife and replaced it in the block. For a moment, he felt there was someone else in the kitchen standing behind him. A presence. He was fearful of turning in case he would have to confront the spectres of the old man and woman that his wife and children had seen. He'd never felt such a chilling, uncanny sensation before.

Slowly he turned. The room was empty, but the feeling of a presence in the house persisted.

He took his cup of tea upstairs to the bedroom. It felt more comfortable than remaining in the kitchen. As he settled into bed again, he decided to leave the bedroom light on while he slept. It felt more secure. Until now, he'd never felt phased by the prospect of darkness since childhood. But rest largely eluded him, as his mind tumbled with all the strange events that had passed.

Billy Parsons was sitting at his desk in the car sales office, scrolling through the company's finances on the computer monitor. His avaricious eyes, set in a bony narrow face, were absorbing every profit and loss, alternating between a gleam and a frown.

Hurst entered the office. Billy looked up.

"Jesus, you look as though you slept in a hedge!" The car dealer greeted his former prison inmate, not realising the accuracy of his observation.

Hurst looked dishevelled and the worse for wear after a night spent beside a hedgerow.

"You're not on the run, are you?" Billy became alarmed. He didn't want the police arriving and linking him with a fugitive from justice.

"No," Hurst assured him, though he knew the police would very much like to speak to him.

He doubted they could discover what he'd done to his parents. People sometimes just disappear. And they'd have some difficulty linking the missing inspector to him. Unless they dredged the lake. But he'd been very careful to cover his tracks. The police could, however, prove he'd been spending his parents' pension money. Bank records would prove it. And with his past prison record, he'd have to serve another term.

"Truth be known, I've got a few gambling debts with a syndicate. They don't leave you with any useful parts if you can't pay up in time," Hurst lied. "I just want to put a bit of space between me and them for a while. They know my own car."

Billy nodded, sympathising with a former partner from Pellridge Prison.

"I've got a nice little motor over there," Billy stood up and crossed to the window overlooking the car sales yard. He pointed to the vehicle.

It was a silver Nissan. From the look of its age and condition it certainly wasn't worth £5,000. However, if you wanted a car in a hurry, without needing to give all your personal details, the premium was naturally higher.

"Here's the registration document. You won't have any trouble getting it through the authorities." Billy handed it over with the car keys. Hurst had absolutely no intention of registering ownership of the vehicle. He just wanted to travel in a car that in the short term wouldn't be flagged up as being associated with him.

"And now the matter of money," Billy approached his friend, who was reaching into his travel bag to take out a wad of notes.

Billy wanted to carry out the transaction quickly. He was planning to offer Hurst coffee and biscuits, and talk over how their fortunes had fared since parting from prison. His former colleague had other plans, which didn't involve socialising.

Hurst had noticed that the office cabin was close to the workshop building where Billy's employees carried out repairs and paint sprays on a mix of vehicles. Many were legitimate, but some of uncertain origin, transformed into a new and dubious life.

Hurst looked out the window towards the workshop, making sure no-one was approaching. In his left hand he held out the bundle of notes for Billy to take. As his former prison mate reached for them, Hurst swung his right fist and smashed him in the face. Billy staggered back with blood beginning to stream from his nose. Hurst followed the attack with another blow to his victim's head. Billy fell back, hitting the side of the desk, then collapsed unconscious on the floor.

Checking again that no-one was coming, Hurst shoved Billy's senseless body into the leg-space enclosure under the desk. From a casual glance it would look as though he was absent from the room for a while. The delay of his discovery before he recovered would give Hurst more time to escape, just in case one of Billy's employees wanted to give chase. He doubted Billy would contact the police. The trader certainly wouldn't want them to pry into his business affairs.

Hurst replaced the money in his travel bag and left the office. The car he'd been 'sold' was not exactly a prize, but it looked innocuous enough for his purposes. He climbed in and drove off.

His first stop was a supermarket 12 miles away. There was now enough distance for Hurst to know he wasn't being followed by any of Billy's men. He bought canned and packet food with a long shelf life. Then he visited a DIY store to buy some equipment for the plan he'd formed, followed by a trip to a clothes shop for a change of appearance.

They were all cash transactions. He didn't want to use a traceable credit card.

Next stop was at a local internet cafe, where he settled in front of a computer for the next stage of his operation, to find a remote retreat that he could rent in the Scottish Highlands.

He selected a few possibilities. Small holiday properties with vacant lets for at least a month. It was out of the peak holiday season, which gave more choice. He noted their locations, in the mountainous Grampian region of the highlands, and the owner contact numbers. Booking online could leave a trace. He'd take a chance one of them would be available when he was nearer to the destination and pay the owner with cash.

Now there was only one other pressing engagement for him.

All the while, a pent-up grudge had been festering and growing inside him. Hurst attributed his current problems to the interfering Paul Hunter. He had convinced himself more and more that the man had discovered something connected to the disappearance of his parents, causing the police to investigate his scam on collecting their pensions.

It might even lead the police to discovering he'd murdered his parents and the inspector. That would put him away for the rest of his life. Hurst's resentment had grown into deep fury. He'd been made a fugitive – and he wanted revenge.

That was the next step in his plan.

Hurst knew from the conversation he'd had with Paul Hunter, that his wife and daughter were staying with Diane's parents at the town of Bridgeworth in Hampshire. He didn't know exactly where, but was about to find out. He drove for 40 miles to reach the town, making for the general hospital serving the area.

He didn't want an image of the car recorded on the CCTV cameras dotted inside the complex, so he parked the car on the road outside. Then he reached for the hooded jacket on the passenger seat, put it on and raised the hood to cover his head. Hurst made his way into the main entrance of the hospital, keeping his face lowered so any prying cameras would not get a clear view of his face.

In a corner of the hospital reception area were three public telephones. He crossed to one of them. It didn't offer any privacy from the bustle of people nearby, so he faced the wall to avoid being heard.

Hurst dialled Paul's mobile number, the one he'd obtained after deliberately leaving a set of keys behind when he'd called at the house.

Paul answered.

"This is Bridgeworth General Hospital," Hurst began in a false voice. "Your wife and children have been involved in an accident. Get here as quickly as possible."

"What's happened?" Paul's distress was palpable.

"We'll let you know as soon as you arrive. But be quick." Hurst hung up.

He crossed reception to a coffee dispenser, then took his drink to a seating area where he could see everyone entering and leaving the building. All the while he kept his face in the shadow of the jacket hood. He picked up a magazine from a nearby table and sat down to wait.

Half-an-hour had passed when he saw a man tearing into reception. It was Paul. This was the moment Hurst had been waiting for. Paul raced to the reception desk, frantically asking the woman behind the counter what had happened to his wife and children. The receptionist took his name and looked through the records.

Hurst rose from the chair and left the building.

The receptionist informed Paul that his family hadn't been brought to the hospital. Deeply relieved, puzzled and angry that someone could have done this to him, to cause so much distress, he left the building and called his wife.

Hurst watched Paul approaching his car and noted the model and registration. He quickly returned to his own vehicle and followed Paul as he drove away. He'd calculated his next stop would be to see his family. Soon he would know exactly where they were staying.

Paul's car pulled up on the driveway of a semi-detached house with a neat front garden. It was situated in a cul-de-sac lined with other semi-detached houses and neat front gardens.

Hurst parked a short distance away and watched as his quarry entered the house. He noted the name and number of his target, 9 Lavender Close. That was all he needed to know for the moment. He drove off.

In preparation for the next stage of his plan, Hurst found a cheap bed and breakfast place to stay in Bridgeworth for the night. He made cash only transactions.

Early next morning he returned to the house in Lavender Close. It was 7.30 and being late in the year, only just growing light.

He drove to the end of the cul-de-sac and noted lights on in the target house. He then drove back down the road a short distance and parked the car so he could make a quick getaway without turning.

The plan was risky, but he was confident of pulling it off. He would go to the house, ring the doorbell and, putting on a hood, force an entry. He knew from what Paul had told him, his wife and daughters were staying there with the grandparents. He hoped Paul would have been re-assured his family were safe by seeing them, and then returned back to his house in Lynthorne.

Hurst was certain he could cope with the elderly couple, as well as the woman and two young girls. But Paul's presence, if he was still there, could cause a problem in resistance.

However, Hurst had a carving knife. If it came to it, he'd finish Paul there and then before escaping. His main plan, however, would be better. The one where Paul – the man he blamed for all his present woes with increasing paranoid intensity – remained alive.

Hurst stayed in the car for a further 10 minutes, thinking through his attack and exit plan. Finally he was ready, about to leave the car, when an immense stroke of luck appeared in the side view mirror. For a moment he couldn't believe it. He wouldn't have to go to the house. His prize objective was approaching him.

He saw two young girls leaving the target residence and walking along the pavement toward his car. They had to be Paul's daughters. It was like a dream come true.

Hurst got out of the car and opened the boot, pretending to be looking for something inside.

As the girls drew near, he leapt out, shoving one roughly backwards so she fell dazed on to the pavement. He grabbed the other girl, Alice, lifted her and dumped her into the boot, swiftly closing the lid.

Her older sister, Rosemary, was disorientated. Everything was happening so quickly. As she got to her feet, Hurst's car had already pulled away and was disappearing round the corner. The girl screamed hysterically.

Neighbours began to stream out their doors, wondering what was causing the commotion.

Hurst could hear banging and yelling from the boot of the car as he made his rapid escape. He needed to quieten his victim as soon as possible, but there were too many cars and people around as he made his way through the town.

It was before rush hour, and he was able to clear the urban area quickly, soon finding a quiet country lane and a small lay-by.

He grabbed the carving knife from the shelf under the steering wheel, got out of the car and opened the boot. It was a pitiful sight. The young girl stared at him with terrified eyes.

"Please let me go! I want my mum!" she pleaded, starting to cry.

Pity was not an emotion familiar to Hurst. No-one had ever shown compassion to him. He placed the knife point against her throat.

"Any noise from you, and I'll stick this in!" He pressed the tip of the blade enough to hurt, but not to cut.

Alice was rigid with horror. Hurst lifted her out of the boot and made her stand.

"Stay there," he ordered and reached inside the boot for a roll of plastic twine. He unravelled a length, sliced it with the knife and tied the girl's hands behind her back. Then he reached for a roll of parcel tape and wrapped it around her head to seal her mouth.

He heard a car approaching and stood to obscure the view of the girl. It passed by. He cut another section of cord to tie her feet. As he did so, he saw her light blue dress was damp and there was liquid on her legs. The poor girl was so terrified, she'd wet herself. So what, he thought, lifted her and dumped her back in the boot, closing the lid.

He smiled to himself. *Now Mr Paul Hunter, you can know what it's like to have the whole world crashing in on you.* The feeling of personal revenge raised Hurst's spirits. He got back into the car and set off for the next destination.

CHAPTER 5

DETECTIVE Inspector Susan Hopkin was at 9 Lavender Close, investigating the abduction. She could see Paul was desperately trying to console his wife, Diane, and 14-year-old daughter, Rosemary.

Their faces were haggard with tears, confused and distraught. The girl was suffering bad bruising down her right side from where Hurst had shoved her harshly on to the pavement. A doctor had checked her, and other than that physical injury she was unharmed. The same could not be said for her mental state, caused by the trauma of seeing her younger sister Alice being violently abducted.

D.S. Hopkin had heard the report of an abduction taking place through a police operations broadcast, and had immediately linked the family's name with her recent visit to Paul.

She had a strong feeling the drama had a connecting thread with Hurst and Inspector George Bird's disappearance. But nothing tangible.

The area was not technically her patch, but a diplomatic call to the local police chief allowed her access to the investigation.

She was keen to question the daughter, Rosemary, for any clue as to the attacker, but for now she was too upset. Any mention of the incident sent her into hysterics.

The girl's grandparents were trying their best to give comfort, while themselves suffering the trauma of their grand-daughter being viciously taken.

D.S. Hopkin was able to interview Jack, the girls' grandfather, who was maintaining the steadiest head in the confusion.

"Poor Rosemary and her mother are in a dreadful state as you can see," he told her, running his hand anxiously over his grey, thinning head of hair while struggling with his own distress.

"She told us it happened so quickly." He was recalling the girl's words immediately after the incident before the deep trauma set in. "He had a big build, but not tall, and dark hair. She thinks he had a coat with a hood, and a silver car, but she can't be sure. It was all so fast."

Jack shook his head in disbelief. The reality of what had happened was still sinking in. "I can't tell you anymore than that, and nor can Rosemary while she's still in shock."

The description of a man with dark hair and strongly built, but not tall, could certainly be applied to Hurst. But then it could be applied to thousands of men. The superintendent had run a check on Hurst's car records while she was travelling to the scene. It was recorded as a red vehicle. Of course, he could have used another car.

"Did Rosemary see the car's registration number," she asked.

"I don't know, I just don't know. You'll have to ask when she's calmed down. I wish we could help more." The man looked tearful. D.S. Hopkin realised this was not the time to put the family under any further pressure, even though it was meant with the best of intentions.

A woman police officer was present, trained in helping families affected by major crimes. For now, that was all that could be done at the house.

The D.S. left to pursue other channels of investigation.

House to house enquiries by officers in Lavender Close and the surrounding area drew a blank. Most people at the time of the incident were in their homes getting ready for the new day. The chance of someone peering out the window or walking down the street at the time of the abduction didn't appear to be a runner.

D.S. Hopkin was convinced Hurst was behind it, but the main suspect had disappeared without trace.

Her next step was to find out which internet providers Hurst used, any phone calls he'd made, money he may have withdrawn from a traceable cash machine and if there was any CCTV footage of him in the area

The superintendent's target had considered these possibilities. Hurst gleaned a lot of useful criminal tips from his time in prison. Especially to strangle Detective Inspector, George Bird, and leave no messy traces of violent death for forensics, rather than his preferred method of hacking with a carving knife.

It was a long drive to Scotland and Hurst had to re-fuel the car a couple of times. Before entering the motorway service stations, his head suitably covered by the hood of his jacket, he stopped briefly on the hard shoulder to warn the girl not to make any noise, or he'd finish her.

Each time, as he opened the boot, he was met by her pitiful frame, bound and hunched. Her eyes staring at him in terror. He didn't particularly care if she died. Her disposal would be an inconvenience to him. But her survival would be a good bargaining chip, if the need arose. He'd try to keep her alive as long as it suited.

He also diverted briefly off the motorway to find a clothes shop.

On the pretext of saying he wanted a surprise birthday present for his daughter, the woman in the shop helped Hurst make the purchase of a pink, cotton dress, based on the rough estimate he gave of his victim's size and height.

He bought it not from sentiment, but because he didn't want to live with the smell of the girl's soiled clothes when he reached his anticipated refuge in the Scottish Highlands.

The late afternoon sun cast long shadows as he neared his preferred destination. The road ran alongside a river with the slopes of mountains rising on either side. He was entering remote territory.

Pulling into a lay-by, he reached into the glove compartment and took out the details of isolated holiday lets in the region that he'd noted down at the internet cafe. He also took out a mobile phone which would not reveal his identity for tracking.

He'd bought a few such phones from a market stall trader near where he lived. They didn't link the caller to a traceable name if used sparingly. Hurst rang a number.

"Andy McIntyre," a man answered.

Using a false name, Hurst explained he was interested in the holiday let Mr McIntyre was advertising on the internet.

"You're in luck," the man replied. "I've had a cancellation. How long do you want it for?"

"A month," Hurst replied.

Andy McIntyre was delighted. That would cover a significant period of the quiet season.

"For you and your family?" he enquired.

"Just me for now. My family will be coming later," Hurst lied.

Mr McIntyre was even more delighted when Hurst offered to pay him cash for the rental.

"Come to my house and I can direct you to the holiday cottage after we've completed our business," McIntyre directed. "It's only five miles away from where I live." He gave the address.

Hurst was constantly concerned the girl in the boot of his car would make a sound and give away her presence, but it was a risk he would have to take.

The road grew narrower and more remote as he made his way to Mr McIntyre's house, climbing a steep mountain track. The old car he'd stolen from Billy Parsons didn't take kindly to the increasingly rough terrain. Nor did poor Alice, crammed in the boot. She was beyond crying, and even began to wonder if she would be better off dead.

Hurst arrived at Andy McIntyre's property, a white bungalow with a slate roof. The owner was an elderly man, dressed in a blue shirt and beige trousers.

He invited his new tenant into a room set aside as his office. The man's wife, Morag, offered their visitor a cup of tea, but Hurst was keen to press on and declined. They completed the transaction and McIntyre volunteered to guide Hurst to the holiday rental by driving ahead in his car.

"It's easy to get lost on the roads round here," he warned.

Hurst once again declined hospitality, fearing at some point his captive in the boot might cry out and reveal her presence. He'd use the satnav to guide himself. He set off and began to feel more relaxed. The hideaway was now a reality.

The car was climbing a steep incline, with an open view to the valley on one side and a mountain crest rising up on the other. Suddenly Hurst became aware of someone sitting on the passenger seat beside him. He turned to look. It was Detective Inspector, George Bird, the officer he'd murdered and despatched to the bottom of the quarry lake.

The detective looked at him with an accusing frown.

Hurst screamed in horror. The car started to swerve off the road. He managed to gain control just as the vehicle was about to plunge over the side and career towards the valley below.

He pulled up, breathless. His heart pounding. The passenger seat was empty.

A police motorcycle patrolman was returning from a call. He'd seen a car a few hundred feet ahead begin to veer off the road, narrowly avoiding a serious accident.

As Hurst was recovering from the shock of seeing the detective inspector he'd killed sitting beside him, he caught sight of a blue flashing light in the side view mirror and the sound of a motorcycle approaching. Had his new location been discovered already? Had the police seen him swerving? Would he have to silence yet someone else?

The motorbike stopped in front of the car. The helmeted officer dismounted and approached. Hurst opened the side window.

"Is there a problem with your car, sir?"

"No, it's fine," Hurst replied

"I saw you nearly swerve off the road."

"I just lost concentration for a moment, spending too much time admiring the beautiful views. I'm sorry," Hurst spun his excuse.

"Is this your car, sir?"

"Yes."

"Can you tell me the registration number?"

Hurst had no idea. He'd briefly glanced at it a few times, but hadn't memorised it. He hesitated.

"I'd like you to step outside of the car, please sir," it was a command couched in a request. He obeyed.

This was a tricky moment for Hurst. He had a carving knife in the passenger glove compartment. No-one else, save his victim in the boot, was present. He could despatch the policeman, but then he'd have another body to deal with.

"I'd like to see your driving licence and insurance," the officer continued to press.

"I've left them at home," Hurst dealt yet another lie.

The officer became more suspicious. He examined the condition of the car.

"Would you please open the boot, sir?" came another veiled command.

That was it. The officer was leaving him no choice.

"The boot release is on the other side," Hurst explained, making his way to the passenger door and the knife in the glove compartment.

Suddenly the police officer's radio burst into life. It was an urgent call to an incident elsewhere.

The officer listened to the details, then looked sternly at Hurst.

"Mind your driving," he warned. "Some of the roads around here are treacherous. I don't want to be called out to scrape you off the ground." He returned to his motorcycle.

Inside the car boot Alice had been able to make out some of the conversation taking place. It gradually dawned on her that Hurst was talking to a policeman. She was gagged so she couldn't shout for help. There was little room to manoeuvre, but she'd managed to twist herself on to her back to kick at the boot lid with her tied feet.

As the began to pound at the lid, the policeman started the motorbike. The deafening roar of the engine, as it sprang into life, muffled all sound of her distress signal.

The noise of the motorcycle receded into the distance, but Alice was desperately hoping she might still be heard by someone who could help. All in vain. Hurst opened the lid and gave her a hard smack across the face. She winced in pain.

"Any more, and you're dead," he pointed his finger threateningly, then slammed the lid shut.

Hurst got back into the car and drove on, relieved at his narrow escape and thinking the fates must be on his side. But the vision he'd seen of the dead inspector deeply troubled him. Was it his ghost coming to haunt him, or was he going insane? His parents had appeared to him too, at the beach.

He dismissed it as imaginings brought on by too much pressure. Now he had the chance to get away from everyone and enjoy some peace, once he'd properly secured his prisoner.

It was growing dark when he arrived at the cosy, white-rendered holiday cottage situated at the end of a narrow gravel track.

The front garden was laid to grass surrounded by a small, stone wall enclosure. Beyond it the grassy terrain sloped gently downwards, before descending steeply toward an expansive lake in the distant valley below.

The landscape at the rear of the cottage rose to a mountain peak, the upper slopes covered in huge swathes of heather.

Hurst hadn't passed another property for miles, and in the fading light he could see no other dwellings in the vicinity. This was the ideal spot for him. He parked the car on a small concrete driveway at the side of the cottage.

His first job was to find suitable accommodation for his prisoner. He looked around the new hideout. There were three bedrooms, but each had a window. They could offer an escape route for his young victim.

The alternative was to keep the girl tied up for the duration of his stay. But he didn't want the inconvenience of untieing her every time she needed the toilet. A secure room would be best. Soon his hope was realised.

There was a windowless storeroom on the ground floor with a lock. It wasn't big, but long enough to fit a single mattress leaving a small space to the side. That would do for her. He hauled a mattress from an upstairs bedroom and dumped it in the storeroom, complete with the luxury of a single blanket. Hurst considered he was being generous.

Back at the car he opened the boot, lifted the girl and carried her into the living room. Alice was beyond struggling, drained and stiff from being hunched for so many hours. She didn't even have the strength to look afraid. Apathy filled her soul.

Hurst told her he was going to remove her bonds.

"But any noise, and I'll kill you," he warned.

Her face was red raw from the tape that he'd wound round her mouth and neck. Her wrists and ankles were badly bruised from the pressure of the cord that had bound them. Her soiled clothes had begun to smell.

"Get that off," Hurst pointed to her dress.

For a moment, totally numbed though she was, Alice suddenly feared she was about to suffer yet more abuse. Fortunately, if Hurst had only one redeeming feature, it was at least possessing no desire for under-age girls. From that she would be safe. But nothing else.

"Get that off and wash yourself in there," he ordered, pointing to the bathroom, which was visible across the hall through the open living room door. He'd checked that it didn't have a window.

"Then put this on," Hurst threw the dress he'd bought for her toward the bathroom door. It fell to the floor. Robotically, devoid of feeling, Alice crossed and picked it up, then went in to wash and change. She'd have to make do without underwear.

While Alice was in the bathroom, Hurst heated some soup in the open-plan living room kitchen. He kept a frequent eye on the bathroom door, in case she tried to slip out and make a bid for freedom.

When the girl came out in her new pink dress, she looked slightly less drawn, but pathetically lost and bewildered.

"I want to go home," she pleaded. "I want my mum and dad," tears streamed down the eleven-year-old girl's face.

Anyone with a spark of humanity would have rushed to comfort her. Unfortunately, Hurst didn't possess such a quality.

"Stop whining," he ordered. "I've made some soup. Sit down," he indicated a seat at the pine table in front of her.

The living room setting would have been cosy for a holiday-maker, with traditional wood furniture, an open brick fireplace and comfortable armchairs. For Alice, it was a place of hell. She obeyed the command to sit, but didn't touch the soup.

"I'm not hungry," she said, staring down at the bowl.

Her welfare was of no consequence to Hurst, other than the fact it could be useful to keep her alive. But she'd survive without food for a while.

"Okay. Follow me." He walked a short distance down the hall and opened the storeroom door. Grabbing her arm, he shoved her inside.

"No noise – or else," he threatened, then turned the key in the lock.

Hurst finished his bowl of soup and soon after went to bed. He left the lights on and his bedroom door open, so he could hear any sound if the prisoner tried to escape. He also wedged a broom under the storeroom door handle to impede any breakout attempt. He was pleased with the progress of his day.

D.S. Susan Hopkin was frustrated. She had no leads on the whereabouts of missing inspector, George Bird, or the young girl Alice.

Forensic examination had found traces of the inspector's hair at Hurst's house, but the detective was known to have visited him on official business, so it demonstrated nothing unusual.

The fact that Hurst's computer was missing had flagged suspicion and, through his internet service provider, Hopkin had details of recent connections he'd made. However, none gave any indication to his present location, or plans he may have been making. And there was no record of any recent cash machine withdrawals.

A general police alert was in place for any sightings of his registered car. But unknown to the detective, that wouldn't reveal any useful clue in the foreseeable future, since the vehicle was at the bottom of the quarry lake.

However, in the absence of finding any clues to his location, the fact he was not leaving any traces of his day to day activities, unlike law abiding citizens, was a marker in itself that either he was dead, or had planned to disappear. D.S. Hopkin tended toward the latter possibility.

Extensive enquiries were also being made to try and locate Alice. So far door to door enquiries had come up with no tangible leads. Nor had the CCTV cameras in and around the town where the girl and her family were staying.

D.S. Hopkin sat in her office studying information on the computer monitor. She was tired and had hardly slept for the last few days. Her time had been filled with visiting or speaking to people who had called with possible leads, all of which proved fruitless.

It seemed she was facing a stone wall, when there came a knock on her office door.

A detective sergeant entered the office. Dan Glover was in his mid-thirties, well-built and wearing a smart, navy blue suit. He sounded excited.

"We've been checking with Hurst's mobile phone company, and we've come up with an interesting number," he announced.

The superintendent had suspected that in Hurst's plan he would now be using a phone that wasn't easy to trace, but she'd ordered a check on any calls made to and from him in recent times.

The detective sergeant pointed to the very last number on the list he'd printed.

"We've traced this to a Billy Parsons. He's got a record for handling stolen cars and was in prison at the same time and place as Hurst."

In Hurst's panic to dispose of the detective inspector and then flee, he'd inadvertently contacted Parsons on his traceable contract phone. He'd since thrown it away so no-one could track it, but the phone had left a clue.

D.S. Hopkin's face brightened.

"Well done!" She congratulated her officer. "This could be our breakthrough."

CHAPTER 6

BILLY Parsons had a dark bruise on the side of his face where Hurst struck him. But he smarted more inside from being double-crossed by a former fellow inmate.

Even though Parsons had been trying to rip him off, in his own world of twisted values, he felt a bond of trust had been broken. He was thinking of a way to try and gain revenge.

The surprise visitors who suddenly arrived in his office had similar desires. But not through any criminal route.

D.S. Hopkin and her detective sergeant, Dan Glover, announced themselves, holding up their identity cards. Parsons almost pissed himself, terrified he was about to be carted off. He worked hard to maintain his outward composure.

"What can I do for you?" he asked with an uncertain smile.

"Where's Edwin Hurst?" the superintendent demanded.

"Who?" Parsons was beginning to regret dealing with his former prison mate. He'd suspected the man was on the run, but getting £5,000 for an old car not worth a fraction of that price had been too tempting. Now he'd not only lost the money and the car, he had the old bill on him into the bargain.

"Oh yes, I remember Edwin Hurst," the car sales director thought he'd better try a different tack. "But I haven't seen him for years. Not since..."

"You were in Pellridge Prison together." Detective Sergeant, Dan Glover, finished the sentence for him.

"Yes, that's right," Billy confirmed.

"Then how come we've got evidence to show he rang and spoke to you a few days ago?" D.S. Hopkin asked.

Billy faltered. If they had proof Hurst had contacted him, what story could he spin?

"Oh yes, I remember now. He just phoned to see how I was getting on," Parsons tried the lie, but knew it didn't sound convincing.

"Look you little shit," D.S. Hopkin was angry. There was so much more at stake than this seedy little man's bent car business. His crimes could wait.

"If you don't tell us right now why he called you, we'll take you in for some serious questioning."

"I've got a business to run," Parsons protested. He was panicking.

"I don't give a toss about your stolen cars, except the one you probably sold or gave to Hurst. Now give me the details of that, and for now we'll leave you alone," the D.S. struck a deal.

Parsons instantly felt happier and compliant.

"Well yes, your right. He did ring me. Asked if he could buy a car," the dealer admitted.

"And did you sell him one?" the detective sergeant pressed.

Parsons told the officers about the visit, but omitted to say the cash transaction was never completed.

"Which car? Give us the details," demanded the superintendent.

Parsons gave all the information they wanted to know about the vehicle.

"Did Hurst say where he was going?" detective Glover quizzed.

"No, I don't know anything else. Whatever he's done, I've no idea. He just drove off." Parsons looked terrified. He didn't want to be linked any further with crimes Hurst might have committed. And from the attitude of the police officers, he gauged it must be something very serious.

D.S. Hopkin had assessed from Parsons' past record that he was nothing more than a small-time criminal. She felt confident he would not get mixed up with abduction and possibly even murder. Without a shred of evidence, she had a gut feeling that was more the mark of Hurst.

For a few days Hurst had enjoyed the peace and quiet of his new Highland home. He'd even managed to take the mile long stroll down to the waters of the lake, or loch as they were called in Scotland. The view was beautiful. Heather uplands rose above the grassy banks on the far side of the water, fading into misty, mountain peaks dominating the distant skyline.

He wished he could spend hours absorbing the sense of freedom he felt after the stress he'd been through in recent days. However, he dared not spend too much time away from his prisoner, in case she found a way to escape in his absence.

Alice was released from her storeroom room cell for sparse meals and bathroom needs, otherwise she remained locked up. She had eaten little and was growing more depressed, fearing she would never see her family again. Her pleas to be released were ignored.

"Please. I won't tell anyone who you are. I won't tell them where you are." she begged him.

"You don't know *who* I am or *where* we are," Hurst replied contemptuously.

It was true, Alice didn't know where she was being held, but it had come back to her that it was the man whose house her parents had bought. She knew she'd seen him before, but it had taken her a little time to remember a visit with her parents to view the property.

Alice said no more and returned to her morose silence, which was fortunate. If Hurst realised for one moment she had recognised him, he would have no other choice but to eliminate her.

Next day, he was preparing breakfast when he heard a car approaching and pulling up outside.

He panicked, looking around for something he could use to attack an unwelcome visitor. He grabbed a kitchen knife and ran to the living room window.

An elderly man was getting out of a car parked behind Hurst's on the concrete driveway. It was Andy McIntyre, the owner who'd rented the cottage to him.

Hurst was greatly relieved it wasn't the police, but concerned the man might start nosing around the property. He replaced the knife in the kitchen, just as the front doorbell rang.

It occurred to him the mattress in the second bedroom was in the storeroom. If McIntyre looked around, he'd wonder why it was missing. Hurst quickly closed the bedroom doors, then unlocked the storeroom. Alice was slumped on the mattress, staring blankly ahead. She glanced at him.

"One sound from you – and you know what will happen!" Hurst's menacing threat needed no further description. He locked the door.

The doorbell rang a second time. Hurst answered.

"Morning," came the cheery greeting from Mr McIntyre, wearing an olive green Barbour jacket. Hurst forced a cheerful greeting in return. As the owner stood there, it was apparent he was expecting to be invited inside.

Hurst surmised it was an inspection visit to ensure he was looking after the property, dressed as a social call. To refuse the man entry would raise suspicions. Reluctantly, he welcomed the owner in.

"Enjoying your stay?" asked the landlord.

"It's a beautiful place." For once the fugitive wasn't lying. He knew the sociable thing would be to offer the visitor a tea or coffee, but he didn't want to prolong the stay.

He could see the man was glancing round, making sure everything was in order. His eye caught sight of a child's dress draped over the back of the sofa.

"You have someone staying with you?" McIntyre enquired.

Hurst had washed and dried the light blue dress Alice was wearing when he'd abducted her. Not out of care, but to be ready if anything happened to the other dress, should he need to take her into a public area for some reason. Now it's presence could undo him. He was considering taking drastic action when he thought of an excuse.

"It's my daughter's. I promised her a holiday," Hurst's fiction began.

"She should be arriving in a day or two. Her mother and myself are separated, but she's letting our daughter stay here for a while."

The answer appeared to satisfy Andy McIntyre.

"Are the bedrooms to your liking?" the landlord walked out of the living room toward the stairway, as if he was about to ascend them. Hurst said they were fine, worried the man might go upstairs and see a mattress was missing.

"While I'm here," McIntyre continued, "do you mind if I check one of the bedrooms? There was some damp coming in. I think I fixed it, but I'd like to see."

This was something Hurst could not risk. McIntyre began to mount the stairs, assuming permission had been granted, without it explicitly being given. He was halfway up when he heard a cry from Hurst, who appeared doubled in pain in the hallway.

McIntyre stopped.

"Are you all right?" the man was concerned and descended the stairs to come to Hurst's aid.

"No, it's okay," Hurst had been bent over and now began slowly to stand upright again. "I've had a lot of back pain recently. I'm hoping a restful break will help put it right," he weaved the story.

McIntyre offered him the address of his doctor for some medication. Hurst politely refused.

"I'll let you get on then. I can take a look at the bedroom another time. Get some rest." The landlord hurriedly made his way to the front door, feeling now that he was intruding on his tenant's right to a peaceful break. "If you need anything, give me a call."

Hurst thanked him and shut the door, grateful that his ruse had worked. It was so much simpler than finding yet another way to dispose of a body.

He went to the storeroom and unlocked the door. Alice was still staring blankly ahead. She looked unwell. But that was fine, he thought, as long as she was alive for possible future use. He locked the door again.

D.S. Hopkin was busy in the police operations room, where officers were examining CCTV footage covering the town and surrounding areas close to Alice's abduction.

Now they had the registration of the car Billy Parson's had sold to Hurst, the investigation was on track again.

The detective was looking at video screen shots of the car travelling through Bridgeworth town, and then taking a road leading into the countryside out of camera range. The video image was too indistinct to see clearly who was driving the vehicle, but Hopkin felt certain it was Hurst.

She'd ordered a general alert to other police forces across the country and gave them details of the road Hurst took out of town. But that, of course, could ultimately lead to anywhere. So far no other sightings of the car had been reported. Information feedback took time and every passing moment left the young girl's life at risk.

Alice's father had told D.S. Hopkin about the hoax call he'd received telling him his family had been involved in an accident. She'd traced the call back from his phone to the telephone paybox in Bridgeworth General Hospital.

CCTV cameras there had recorded a man wearing a hood making the call. The build of the caller fitted Hurst, but there was no distinct image of his face. Other shots showed the man moving in a way that looked like he was shadowing Paul. Then he left the hospital grounds and disappeared out of view from the cameras.

Once again, the detective was absolutely certain it was her prime suspect, but she had no firm proof. Fingerprints left by Hurst on the phone would have been obliterated by now, with possibly hundreds of other callers using the handset since. And similarly, any of his DNA would have been wiped out.

The news of Alice's abduction had been reported in the media, but until now D.S. Hopkin had been reluctant to give details about her main suspect to the public, fearing it could hinder the investigation. Her greater fear was that it might also drive Hurst in panic to dispose of the child.

He may even have killed her by now, but if she was still alive, the superintendent didn't want to be the instrument of her demise.

However, time was running out. The detective's next move would be to ask Alice's parents to make a televised plea for information.

Paul Hunter and his family were still struggling to cope with the shock of their daughter being violently snatched from their lives.

He was staying with them at the grandparents' house where police officer Anne Watts was assigned on special duties to offer the family support.

D.S. Hopkin had a generally resilient nature, but the distress the family was enduring penetrated even her cynical shell when she arrived. It was important to keep a mental distance from suffering in her work, but sometimes it was difficult to avoid.

Diane, and daughter Rosemary, looked drained from worry and tears. Paul was exhausted trying to maintain a confident attitude for his family and stop them sinking into utter despair. Inside he was suffering the same abject fear for Alice's safety.

Detective Hopkin decided Paul would be the one to approach and suggest he and his wife appear in a TV broadcast to the nation. She thought the sight of their distress might encourage anyone hiding Hurst to have second thoughts and give him up. She drew Paul aside from comforting his wife and daughter to have a quiet chat.

"If the public see you and your wife, I think it will encourage someone to give us valuable information," the superintendent explained.

"But if Hurst has taken Alice, he might do something..." he paused not wanting to say the awful thought in his mind. "He might do something...drastic."

Hopkin assured him a televised appearance would only help, though inside she knew it was a potential risk. But doing nothing could be even worse.

Paul was driven by trying anything that could help ensure his daughter's safe return. He realised too there could be risks. The choice was limited. He spoke to his wife and they agreed to make a televised appeal.

A photograph of Hurst, taken from his prison days, and images of Alice were publicised in the hope someone may have spotted them.

The result was a flood of calls to the police from people all over the country saying they'd seen Hurst and Alice since she'd been snatched. The only problem was the sightings were all mostly within a few hours of each other. They couldn't possibly have travelled from one end of the country to the other in a matter of hours. It would be a long sifting process. But it was a new start.

A day later, D.S. Hopkin received a call from a service station manager on the M6 motorway near Manchester, two hundred miles north from where Alice had been abducted. He said his staff had been replaying a CCTV video of their petrol station forecourt, after it was suspected someone had driven off without paying for their fuel.

On part of the video they'd noticed another man filling his car nearby, with his coat hood covering his head and keeping his face down, as if attempting to hide his identity. It had seemed a bit suspicious to his staff.

They'd picked him up on a clearer CCTV video when he entered the forecourt kiosk to pay for the petrol in cash. For a moment his hood slipped off his head and revealed his face. The service station manager wasn't sure, but his staff thought it looked very much like the man the police were after in the abduction case.

The manager emailed a video clip to Hopkin. She sat at her desk examining it on the computer screen. It wasn't a sharp image, but in freeze frame she was ninety percent sure the video showed Hurst.

A group of detectives dedicated to the case, crowded round her desk. All of them let out a cry of triumph as they saw the image. At last a breakthrough. Their target was headed north. The service station forecourt shot of the car and registration matched the vehicle Hurst had bought from Billy Parsons.

The first major clue was quickly followed by another call and video clip sent on from a woman who owned a clothes shop further north in the Cumbrian town of Penrith. The CCTV camera in her shop captured images of Hurst with his hood down, while he bought a dress for his 'daughter', the owner explained.

The focus of the investigation had now gained new impetus, as police forces in the north of the country were alerted to be on the lookout for any sightings of Hurst and his young victim.

But time passed, and nothing came in to confirm any information pointing to the suspect's location in the Scottish Highlands.

CHAPTER 7

ALICE sat at the dining table in the cottage, picking at a plate of tinned spaghetti Hurst had heated on the calor gas hob. She had no appetite.

For the first time since he was a boy, Hurst had experienced a distant sense of emotional caring, deep in his soul. He was beginning to feel the merest pang of sympathy for the girl. His blind vendetta against her father had been rolled into vengeance on the whole family. This extreme prejudice was fracturing slightly.

He began to see Alice as someone entirely in her own right. No longer connected with the blame for his present difficulties. But his irrational mind was fighting to keep her linked with the problem. Otherwise guilt and sorrow for her would cause his resolution to fall apart.

Until now, Hurst hadn't even tried to speak to Alice, other than give orders. He was feeling more relaxed as he sat at the table with her and, in a clumsy way, tried to engage her in conversation.

"I don't know your name? What is it?" he asked brusquely.

Alice glanced at him, but didn't answer. She had nothing to say. She hated him.

"Are you a mute?" Hurst knew she wasn't through her pleas for release, but he was annoyed by her response.

"I want to go home. Why have you done this? I've never done anything to you," Alice replied.

Hurst considered telling her, but it was pointless, She was a child. She wouldn't understand.

He was about to take a mouthful of spaghetti when he suddenly froze. Slowly he turned his head left. Sitting on another chair at the table was his father, frowning at him. Hurst dropped the forkful of spaghetti.

He turned right and saw his mother. His jaw dropped in terror.

"Get out, get out! You're dead!" he screamed, knocking his chair backwards as he rose in panic.

Then his eye caught someone standing opposite him behind Alice. It was the deceased inspector, George Bird.

"You're all bloody dead!" Hurst raged. "Leave me alone!"

He ran to the kitchen counter and grabbed a knife, turning back to confront his unwelcome visitors.

Alice sat at the table, horrified. She could only see Hurst in the room. He rushed toward the inspector, stabbing wildly at him with the weapon.

Alice jumped out of the chair and ran to a corner of the room, sinking to the floor and cowering as Hurst thrust the knife repeatedly into thin air. He turned to confront his parents, knife poised high to attack again. Alice feared for her life. Then Hurst stopped, remaining motionless for a moment. His ghosts had disappeared.

Cautiously he turned his head, gazing round the room, his eyes frightened and searching. He looked at the girl. Alice was staring at him, petrified. Was he going to kill her? *He's totally insane,* she thought.

Hurst placed the knife on the dining table, re-assuring himself that all the stress of the past few days had caused him to hallucinate. He picked up the chair he'd knocked over, then walked toward Alice.

"Get into your bedroom!" Still cowering, she rapidly made her way to the storeroom, feeling an ambiguous sense of security as he locked her inside.

The televised appeal by Paul Hunter and his wife, Diane, was broadcast on the late afternoon news bulletins. At the time, Andy McIntyre, the owner of the cottage occupied by Hurst, had been working outside on the smallholding that surrounded his home.

It kept him and his wife, Morag, self sufficient in vegetables, eggs and poultry for much of the year. Their retirement income was also supplemented by rent from the cottage he rented to holidaymakers.

The property was once the home of his sister, Anne. When she had died five years earlier, a widow without children, he converted it for the purpose of letting.

Inside the McIntyre's own modest two-bedroomed house, the television was on in the living room. Morag was busy dusting her treasured ornaments of animals and figurines on the sideboard. She heard the Hunter's appeal and listened to the details of the man that police were trying to trace.

She felt deeply for the family, and if she could, she would dearly love to help. Except she was blind. So she couldn't see the photograph of Hurst displayed on the TV screen, or match in her mind the description given by the news presenter. She couldn't possibly know she'd offered a cup of tea to the fugitive when he'd arrived at the house to pay for the let.

Morag knew her home and everything placed in it. Household chores presented no problem. But the outside world had disappeared from view since she had gone blind twenty years ago.

Morag told her husband about the televised appeal when he returned from his work on the smallholding. He sympathised, then went off to bath. He hardly watched television and in the evening he read to his wife before they went to bed.

Had he needed to go into the local village of Cullness the next day, he would have seen the papers in the newsagent's shop displaying Hurst's photograph on the front pages, with the make and registration of his car. But Mr McIntyre only went into the village once a week, and his next visit wasn't due for another five days.

Hurst stepped outside the holiday cottage. His fear and anger had dissolved since the uncanny visitation of his parents and the inspector.

Although convinced the episode was stress-induced pure imagination, he was terrified they might re-appear at any time. They seemed so real.

The temperature had plunged overnight and he shivered as the cold hit him. The coat he'd brought in his rush to escape was designed for warmer weather.

Grey, heavy clouds hid the sky and hugged the crests of the mountains. Flecks of snow swirled in the air. The Scottish Highlands were prone to early snowfall as winter approached.

Hurst liked to walk each day, the keen freshness of the upper slopes cleared his mind, relaxed him. By the time he returned to the cottage, the snow was growing heavier. A fine coating had already covered the ground.

Inside he made a coffee and turned on the radio. There was a television, but it wasn't working. He was reluctant to prevail on another visit from Andy McIntyre or have an engineer fix the set. He preferred the safety of solitude. So he left it.

He sat down in the armchair to drink his coffee and listen to the music on the radio. He'd check on his captive in the storeroom shortly.

After a few minutes the music was interrupted by a news bulletin.

"Police have received new information in the search for missing 11-year-old schoolgirl Alice Hunter. She was abducted near her grandparent's home in Bridgeworth, Hampshire last Tuesday morning," the announcer began.

"Edwin Hurst, who is being sought by police in connection with the incident, has been seen on CCTV video footage showing him travelling north into Cumbria. He may possibly be in the town of Penrith or local area. People in the region are asked to report any sightings of him or the girl to police. But the public are warned not to approach Hurst, as he is believed to be dangerous."

The announcer went on to give details of the wanted man's make of car and registration number.

For a moment Hurst couldn't move. He was locked in horror. He'd taken such care to mask his escape. How did they know the direction he'd travelled in? Then he thought of the stops. The garage. But he'd had his hood up. Ah, the clothes shop. Stupidly he forgot to put the hood over his head. The shop must have had a camera.

But the car and registration number? That bastard, Billy Parsons, must have given the details to the police. That's how they traced his route. Hurst vowed to kill the man next time he saw him.

At least the police hadn't traced him to Scotland. But what if the owner of the cottage had seen or remembered the car registration? McIntyre and his wife had also seen him. The police must have issued a photo of him. Perhaps he would need to pay them a visit.

Hurst, of course, was unaware that Andy McIntyre and his wife had no idea of his implication in the crime. Or that the woman was blind. He rose from the armchair and looked out the window, wondering if it was time to move on. The falling snow had thickened and he could barely see anything outside.

He slept restlessly that night, fearful the cottage owner may have informed the police of his location. As the morning light seeped into the bedroom, he began to feel more secure. If McIntyre had informed the police, they would surely have arrived by now. He got out of bed and peered through the bedroom window.

The snow had stopped and everywhere was covered in a thick layer of glistening white. The mountain peaks beyond were magnificently highlighted against the clear blue sky.

Hurst heated vegetable soup for breakfast. Alice sat at the dining table. Her hair was matted. She had no inclination to care how she looked. Nor did she have the use of any toiletries other than a complimentary bar of soap in the bathroom.

She spooned her soup apathetically. Her mind had no appetite, but her stomach yearned sustenance.

After they'd eaten, Hurst ordered Alice back to her storeroom cell. Then he put on his coat and stepped outside on to the crisp snow. He loved to see fresh snowfall. It was virginal, pure, always bestowing beauty even to the mundane and ugly. How he wished it could reach inside to purge his dark, troubled soul.

The loch waters below looked stunning. A huge expanse of blue, cradled by the dazzling slopes.

His car was buried under the snow. Any snooping eyes would not see the registration, though he doubted any visitors would get through on the mountain roads at present. He set off for a walk, making slow progress as his feet sank deeply with every step.

Alice sat on her bed. She'd heard Hurst close the front door and then silence. The strange man holding her prisoner seemed to spend a lot of time outside the cottage. She had no idea what he was doing.

Every time he banished her to the makeshift prison, she heard the dreaded turn of the key, reinforcing her sense of captivity. This time, she was sure she hadn't heard the key turning. Alice had wondered many times how she might escape. The four walls of the room offered no openings, and Hurst's wary eyes were ever watchful when she was let out.

Had he left the door unlocked on this occasion?

Alice rose from the bed and turned the door handle, pulling it toward her. It opened! He'd forgotten to lock it.

She entered the living room on tiptoe, fearing Hurst might just be resting and she'd wake him. Alice looked in his bedroom. It was empty. He was out. Alice went to the window in the living room and saw the deep coating of snow. She hand no notion of where she was, or to where she could immediately escape. Only the strong urge to get away.

She needed to act quickly. Her captor might return any moment. Then her eyes caught sight of a phone on the table. She could ring for help. The girl picked up the phone. The battery was low and there was no signal. She howled in frustration. The only course was to go outside and see if she could get better reception.

Alice tried to open the front door. It was locked. She returned to the living room window. It too was locked. She tried all the other windows. They were all locked. Alice decided she would have to smash one open and crawl out. It would be noisy, but there was no other choice.

She went to the kitchen. In her brief periods of release, she'd seen a heavy, wooden cutting block in there. She hoped it would have enough weight to smash the window if she could swing it hard enough. As she approached the block, resting on the counter, she caught sight of a key hanging on a hook. It looked like a door key. She grabbed it, praying it was a spare.

Fortune was on her side. Alice inserted the key into the front door lock and it turned. She pulled and the door opened.

The cold air struck as Alice stepped outside clutching the phone. She wore open-toed shoes, the one's she'd been wearing when she was violently stolen away, and was covered only by a flimsy cotton dress. The snow reached almost to the knees of her small frame, but the feeling of freedom drove out any feeling of the chill.

She saw footsteps in the snow leading away from the cottage. They could only be those of her accursed captor. The youngster looked around to be certain he wasn't anywhere in sight, then made her way down the slope of the mountain away from the direction of Hurst's tracks.

Alice travelled for several hundred feet, frequently checking to see if the phone had picked up a signal and hoping she might come to a road where she could flag a passing car.

She passed between a cluster of snow covered bushes, grateful for the protection it gave from possibly being seen by Hurst. Then her wish to find a road was granted, as further down the slope she saw the curve of a narrow lane. But hopes of seeing passing cars were dashed. Drifts of snow blocked the route and only a snow plough could carve a way through.

Hurst approached the cottage. The walk had refreshed him and he was looking forward to a snack of coffee and biscuits. For a moment he thought it was an illusion as he neared the cottage door. It seemed to be half open. Then he realised it really was. He knew he'd shut and locked it.

He stumbled in panic through the snow to reach the door. No cars had arrived. Perhaps the owner had walked there to see if he was okay. Had McIntyre found his captive?

Hurst called out as he reached the door, pushing it open. No reply. He entered and saw the storeroom door open. His prisoner had flown. But how? He must have forgotten to lock it. Stupid. But the front door had been locked. He checked in the kitchen and saw the spare key was missing. *Bitch.*

But worse. His phone wasn't on the dining table. The girl had taken it and could be ringing the police right now! Hurst had begun to warm to her. He'd even started to think that he might invite her to go on walks with him. He believed in his twisted way she was beginning to like him. He'd fed her. Kept her alive. Now she'd betrayed him.

Stepping outside again, Hurst quickly saw Alice's tracks in the snow. They were small impressions. Obviously it was her. He followed her trail as speedily as he could, slipping several times in pursuit.

Alice remembered her father's phone number because part of the sequence contained her birth date. But after several attempts to ring him on Hurst's mobile, it had failed to connect. She hadn't considered ringing the police, because she wanted her dad. She had no idea he was nearly 600 miles away.

She held up the phone and took a photo of the scene in front of her and then began typing a message. A faint reception signal appeared. She got as far as inputting *hel...* when she heard a sound from behind. Alice turned. Hurst was bearing down on her, a murderous look in his face. The girl tapped 'Send' on the screen.

With all his force, Hurst pushed the youngster backwards. Alice hit the ground, crying in pain and saved only from serious injury by the snow absorbing most of the impact.

The phone flew out of her hand and skidded across the icy covering. Hurst approached and stamped on it furiously, driving it through the snow layer until it was crushed on the hard ground beneath.

In the same moment he regretted his stupidity. Now he wouldn't be able to check the call log and see if the girl had contacted someone. He grabbed Alice's arm and pulled her up.

"Who did you ring?" he demanded venomously.

"No-one," she trembled, looking terrified.

Hurst smacked her face.

"You're lying. Tell me!"

"I didn't, I didn't speak to anyone. There was no signal," she prayed he'd accept her word.

It was true, thought Hurst. Reception in the area was patchy.

He hadn't been able to detect a signal on the occasions he'd tried, which was only briefly. He didn't want to give any trace of his location to interceptors. However, he felt safe with the anonymous phones he'd bought back home from the market trader.

Although Hurst believed the girl, he was furious that she'd attempted to escape. He scooped her under his arm and effortlessly carried her back up the mountain slope, anger driving his powerful physique. She would suffer for what she had done. No food or drink for two days.

Alice's father was working in a makeshift office set up in the house of his parents-in-law. He was trying to keep his business together, because even as the family's world was falling apart, the bills would keep coming. Whatever might be the dreadful outcome, he was compelled to continue looking after his wife and their daughter, Rosemary.

His clients expressed their deepest concern at the news of Alice's abduction, and offered him all the time in the world to concentrate on finding her. But Paul knew, as a freelance, he would soon lose custom if delayed projects affected their own business. They'd go elsewhere.

He had difficulty concentrating on the work. It had become a mere mechanical process, and he was about to stop and spend time comforting his wife and daughter again. Then his phone alerted him to a message.

His eyes widened as he looked at the contents. A snow covered scene and letters beneath spelling *hel...*

Instinctively he knew it was from his missing daughter. His blood ran cold. She'd tried to text '*help*' he was certain. Hope filled him. She was still alive. He dialled the registered number, but it rang without answer.

Quickly he got up to tell his family and the police officer giving them support. Then he stopped.

The thought came that if the police rounded on Hurst in a heavy-handed way, the maniac might kill her. He dearly wanted to share the news with his wife and daughter, but they could become even more distressed if they saw what he believed was a desperate plea for help from Alice.

Paul looked at the photograph again and decided his daughter must have been taken abroad. There was snow. Perhaps she'd been abducted to the continent, Switzerland, Austria or Germany. Countries more prone to early winter weather.

Then he remembered he'd heard on the news that Scotland had experienced earlier than usual snowfall, while the south of Britain remained mild.

He studied the photo. It contained a nameplate sign beside a snowbound road. He couldn't read it. He loaded the photo on to his laptop and increased the magnification. The lettering on the sign was mostly obscured by snow. The end section was blurred and slightly pixelated, but he could make out the letters ...*t-i-l-l-o-c-h*. It had the hallmark of a Scottish name.

Paul did a Google search for places in Scotland ending with the same letters. He found a village called Glentilloch. It seemed to be the most likely match.

Next he studied satellite mapping of the area. There were no ground level views available, the setting being too remote to include on street mapping. So he couldn't match the sign with the image Alice had sent. But he was certain she must be somewhere in that area.

Had she taken the photo where she was being held? From the abrupt message, it seemed she may have escaped, but was stopped in flight. Paul needed to act fast.

He entered the living room where his wife and daughter sat on the sofa talking to the police support officer.

"I need to pop out for a while and meet a client. I won't be long," Paul spun an excuse. He put his hands on Diane and Rosemary's shoulders. "It's all right. We'll get Alice back safely," he assured them and kissed their heads.

He left and got into his car, pulling swiftly away for the destination in Scotland. At a push he could be there in six or seven hours. He was going to run that bastard Hurst to ground. Kill him if necessary.

Paul had been driving for five hours and noticed the car was running low on fuel. He pulled into a motorway service station to refill. His wife and daughter would be getting worried about his absence. He gave Diane a call.

"Sorry darling, but I've been delayed. I'm likely to be late." He lied for what he believed to be the best of intentions. "I'll stay at our house for the night and give you a call first thing tomorrow. If you hear anything call me."

Diane was not happy, though accepted he must keep his work going. But she would never want to spend another night in that accursed, haunted property, which she blamed for the start of their present ills.

The woman police officer looking after Diane and Rosemary had a feeling of disquiet about Paul's absence. It didn't seem to fit that in such a difficult time he would leave his family alone overnight for the sake of business.

She made an excuse she needed to fetch something from the car, and left to call Detective Superintendent Hopkin. The senior officer initiated a trace on Paul's call to his wife and a log of any other calls he had recently made or received. She told the support policewoman to return to the house and not tell the family what was happening.

Hopkin and Detective Sergeant, Dan Glover, were at their computers in the office, sifting through statements taken from members of the public.

The call about Paul's absence put them in a quandary.

"You don't think he had anything to do with the abduction, do you?" the detective sergeant posed the question.

D.S. Hopkin thought for a moment.

"I didn't feel that from his body language. He looked totally distraught," she ventured. "Unless, of course, he's a bloody fantastic actor. But I don't think he's part of it."

"Then what's he up to?"

"He might really have been delayed by business," Hopkin replied. "It could simply be the truth."

"There's something else," the sergeant was struggling for a different solution. He reached for the mug of coffee on his desk and took a sip.

D.S. Hopkin paused from sifting through the statements, and sat back in her chair as a possibility struck.

"I wonder if he's been contacted by Hurst?" she voiced her thoughts. "If they've arranged some kind of deal."

Sergeant Glover nodded agreement with the feasibility.

"Hopefully the trace on his call will give us some idea. That is, if the trackers bloody well get on with it." Hopkin picked up the desk phone to discover how the search was progressing.

She spoke, then slammed the phone down.

"They've got a technical fault. It'll be at least another fucking hour!"

The sky was beginning to darken when Paul neared his destination in the Scottish Highlands.

The snow level grew deeper as he ascended the mountainous terrain. Fortunately the snow ploughs had been busy. The main road was accessible. The satnav had directed him toward the village he'd seen in the photo message, but now it could be tricky as he turned off the main route to where the ploughs hadn't been at work.

Paul was partly lucky. A local farmer had been out with a mechanical shovel clearing the road, but it had left a treacherous layer of ice. The car slipped and skidded several times, nearly careering into the heaped snow banks on either side. The steep, upward slope added to the difficulty.

Paul decided he would have to abandon the vehicle and walk. He was losing precious time and becoming desperately frustrated with the slow progress. The sun had set and twilight was fading. He took the aerial photo of the area he'd copied off the internet, and a torch from the boot.

As he began walking, the slippery ice underfoot hindered progress yet further. Twilight turned to darkness, but the white sheen of the snow brightened the surroundings. With the aid of the torch, Paul could see a reasonable distance ahead, but cold now started to penetrate the light trousers and jacket he was wearing.

He saw the silhouette of a signpost and approached. In the torch beam it read *Glentilloch*. The snow covering part of the sign in Alice's photo message, had since fallen away. Paul repositioned himself to try and find the spot where the photo had been taken. It led to a steep bank of snow on the side of the road. He would have to climb it to marry up the angle of the photo.

Frequently slipping as he struggled to get a grip on the icy surface, he climbed to the top. The photo had been taken near this spot. Beyond, there was an upward slope, and in the torchlight he saw an opening between a cluster of bushes about 20 feet ahead.

Then Paul caught sight of an area a short distance away where the snow cover had been disturbed by footprints and possibly something dragged around. He approached.

On the internet aerial mapping he'd studied, there was a cottage located not far from this location. A few hundred yards or so beyond the bushes. He felt a surge of hope that he may have located where Alice was being held.

The message she'd sent had the hallmark of an interrupted text. Had she escaped from the cottage and taken the photo? From the marks in the snow, it seemed there could have been some sort of struggle. Perhaps Hurst had found her? But how could she have taken a photo? Her own phone was still at home.

As the last thought crossed his mind, the torchlight fell on what looked like the broken remains of a red mobile phone. Heavy impressions in the snow indicated it had been crushed underfoot.

Paul saw more footsteps leading away from the scene toward the path through the bushes. He followed them upwards and soon saw lights shining in the windows of a cottage. His heart began to pound furiously. Something told him his daughter was being held a prisoner inside. Now was the time to act.

He had to rescue Alice. But he was likely to meet violent opposition. How could he lure his enemy into a trap without putting his daughter's life in any greater danger?

After waiting for two hours, D.S. Hopkin was about to call the technical team for the third time, when the phone rang.

"We've traced the calls," came the man's voice. "We're emailing the details now."

Dan Glover looked over Hopkin's shoulder as the information came up on her computer screen.

The traces showed Paul had called his wife from a service station in Cumbria. That was over 200 miles away, and nowhere near the couple's home where he said he'd be staying overnight.

Then the superintendent saw the trace on the message sent to Paul's phone. It came via a transmitter in the Scottish Highlands. It covered a wide area, but the population in the region was sparse.

The technical team had been able to access the photo sent to Alice's father with the unfinished text for help, though there was no trace as to the owner of the phone. But the detectives' thinking was on the same lines as Paul. It didn't take them long to deduce the locality and high possibility Alice was being held near there.

Now D.S. Hopkin faced the problem of having no authority to take charge of investigations in that part of the country and she couldn't get there quickly without flying. She would have to alert the police commander for the region in Scotland.

Hopkin rang the force's headquarters and spoke to the chief, impressing on him the urgency of the situation. He was well aware of the national hunt for Hurst, but D.S. Hopkin was met with bad news.

"There's a force ten storm approaching that area. It'll create hazardous, blizzard conditions," the commander told her. "I have an experienced team of officers able to cope with tough conditions, but they'll have to go in on foot. It will be impossible to get in by helicopter for several hours."

"Do what you can," Hopkin pleaded, "because the girl's life is in great danger."

"Well do everything possible," the chief reassured, and agreed to the superintendent's request that she be allowed to join the search as soon as she could arrive.

Hopkin replaced the phone and turned to her sergeant.

"Contact transport and arrange for a helicopter to fly us to Scotland."

CHAPTER 8

A CHILL wind began blowing as Paul grappled with an idea to gain entry to the cottage. He was convinced his daughter, Alice, was being held there by Hurst.

He could try knocking on the door. There was the possibility some innocent family might be living there. But if it was Hurst, he'd immediately be alerted. Paul needed first to identify his quarry.

Inside the cottage Hurst was at the dining table eating yet more tinned soup, accompanied by a diminishing supply of cheese crackers. Alice was locked in the storeroom. She would get no food tonight, or even perhaps for the next day or two, as punishment for trying to escape.

Hurst raised another spoonful of soup to his mouth, then dropped it in horror, the liquid spattering his shirt. Sitting in the dining chairs on each side of him at the table were his deceased mother and father, and opposite him, the dead police inspector, George Bird.

"You've done terrible things, Edwin," his mother frowned, wagging her finger at him.

"I told you he'd amount to no good," his father smugly announced, shaking his head in despair.

"You will pay for this!" the inspector rose from his seat, pointing in accusation at Hurst, the threatening glare in his face slowly dissolving into a hideous skull, staring coldly at him.

Hurst yelled at them, jumping out of his chair. "Get away! You're not real!" He began to back away. The spirits approached him.

"For God's sake leave me alone!" Hurst lifted a chair.

"You murdered us!" the ghosts screamed.

Hurst hurled the chair. It cascaded across the dining table, sweeping the soup bowl on to the floor, as it hurtled toward his deathly accusers. The missile passed through them, smashing into the far wall and collapsing in a heap of broken wood.

Undeterred, the spirits glided venomously on to their target.

"Stop, or I'll kill the girl," Hurst threatened. He ran to the kitchen and picked up a knife.

Alice could hear her captor's ranting. She was terrified and curled herself into a ball on the mattress, sticking her fingers in her ears to blot out the dreadful sound of the madman. Any second she expected him to burst in and kill her in a raging frenzy.

Outside the cottage, her father scooped a handful of snow and rolled it into a hard snowball. He was sheltering behind a bush about 15 feet from the property. He drew back his right arm and aimed it at a window close to the front door. It impacted with a heavy thud and shattered into pieces.

Hurst's ghosts were almost upon him when the snowball struck. In a split second the spectres disappeared. The sound of the impact brought Hurst swiftly back to present reality. He turned to the window, his heart still pounding from the unearthly visitation, and now increasing from the fear that earthly visitors may have caught up with him.

But quickly he reassured himself that no-one could have discovered his hideaway. He'd been so careful to hide his tracks.

He crossed to the window and drew back the curtains a little. The snow reflected enough light for him to make out the nearby surroundings. No-one was in sight. But obviously something must have hit the window.

Then he noticed a small, accumulation of ice stuck to the window pane. It reminded him of the impression a snowball would leave hitting glass. Only a human could have thrown that. Though hardly the method of a call by police.

Paul had ducked back behind the bush after delivering the missile. He peered out cautiously. After a few moments the curtains drew back. That was it. He could see Hurst standing there, peering out. Paul waited. Soon the curtains were drawn again. Now he knew he was on target, and could move on to his next plan of action.

He stepped out from behind the bush and approached the front door. He beat loudly on it with his hand.

"Hello. Anyone at home? I've been hiking and lost my way. Please help?" he called out.

He anticipated the moment the door opened, he would rush Hurst and overpower him in a surprise attack. Kill him if necessary in order to rescue his daughter. However, he was a simple architect. Hurst was an accomplished killer.

Paul suddenly heard a sound to his right. He turned to be met by the sight of a fist flying into his face. Then nothing.

Hurst had suspected an unwelcome visitor might be trying to trick him, and had slipped out the back and round the side of the property, creeping up silently in the snow.

The attacker looked down on his floored opponent, the man he hated. The one who had visited all this trouble on him. He marvelled at his good fortune. The fact that this stupid man had personally delivered himself for the ultimate execution Hurst had planned for him. It was to have been through a hostage trade for his daughter. Except now he wouldn't have to trade. He could just kill and dispose of them both. No witnesses.

Hurst opened the front door, grabbed Paul's legs, and pulled him down the hallway into the living room.

Paul was starting to stir. Hurst grabbed the carving knife he'd placed on the table after using it to fend off his ghostly persecutors just moments before. Paul looked up as his captor approached. In terror, he saw Hurst raise his right arm, clenching the knife, ready to plunge the blade into him. He rolled across the floor and sprang to his feet preparing to defend.

Hurst rounded on him, then suddenly stopped. It occurred to him that if this man had discovered his hideaway, the police would soon discover it too.

Still clenching the knife, Hurst quizzed his captive. "How did you find me?"

Paul remained silent.

"Your daughter. You got a message from her, didn't you?" Hurst remembered the girl using his phone.

"Where is she?" Paul demanded. "You can do anything you like with me, but for God's sake, let her go. She's done nothing wrong."

Hurst wasn't interested in the man's act of bravado or pleas for his daughter. Evading capture was his only thought.

"Have you told the police where I am?" he demanded.

"No. I wasn't sure myself until now," Paul didn't want to panic him into a knee jerk reaction. "I just came to offer myself as a hostage in exchange for freeing my daughter."

Hurst had no desire to bargain with his new captive, but decided the father and daughter could be useful to him. It was time to move on. A new plan sprang to mind.

With a threatening wave of the knife, he ordered Paul to walk into the hallway and toward the storeroom. He unlocked the door and pushed it open, beckoning his captive to enter.

Alice looked up from her bed, overjoyed at suddenly seeing her father standing there.

"Daddy, daddy," she cried, springing up to see him.

Paul was equally thrilled to see his daughter alive and turned to embrace her. In the same moment Hurst roughly shoved the girl's father into the room, catching him off-balance so that he fell on to the bed.

Hurst grabbed Alice by the arm and pulled her away, swiftly closing and locking the door. As he dragged her down the hallway to the living room, he could hear Paul calling out, hammering on the storeroom door.

"Let me out! For Christ's sake, don't hurt her!"

Hurst ignored the plea and took out a length of rope he stored in the kitchen drawer. He used it to tie Alice's hands behind her back. She was terrified, and now also fearful for her father's life. She wished she'd never sent him the message. It had obviously drawn him into a trap.

Her imprisoner gathered some packaged food and put it in his travel bag. Then he shoved the girl back down the hall to the storeroom and unlocked the door.

Paul was about to attack, but saw Hurst holding the blade of the knife at his daughter's throat.

"I'm sorry daddy," Alice cried pitifully.

"It's all right my love," he reassured, reaching out to comfort her.

"Shut up! Keep back!" Hurst shouted, moving the point of the knife closer to Alice's throat.

Her father obeyed. He was going to overpower this heartless bastard even if it was his last act, but he couldn't risk his daughter's life. An opportunity would arise.

Hurst ordered Paul to carry his travel bag and open the front door. They stepped out into the freezing night air. A strong wind was beginning to blow with the cold sting of snowflakes hitting their faces.

"Let me cover her," Paul pleaded. "She'll freeze to death." He put down the travel bag and took off his jacket, placing it around Alice's shoulders. Hurst held the knife ready to attack if the girl's father tried any tricks. Then he handed Paul a torch to light the way, while keeping the weapon in his other hand pointed at Alice.

"Over there," Hurst commanded, waving the direction and holding the girl by her right arm. They began walking through the deep snow. The route took them down the slope of the mountain.

During his walks, Hurst had noticed a rowing boat moored to a small jetty at the lake below. He'd also seen a cottage on the far side of the waters. If the police were closing in on his hideaway, as he strongly suspected, a temporary one-night stay elsewhere might keep him safe a little longer while he worked out a permanent means of escape.

The snow was thickening, the driving wind increased and visibility began to deteriorate. Although Alice had her father's coat around her, the flimsy cotton dress she wore offered no protection from the freezing temperature. She began shaking uncontrollably.

The torchlight became useless for guiding them, as the blinding weather intensified.

Hurst forced the girl and her father onward down the slope. It would lead to the loch at the bottom, but heaven knows if they'd arrive at the moored boat. Assessing direction had become impossible.

They struggled on for half-an-hour, though it seemed hours had passed, when they reached the lake shoreline. Ice was forming around its perimeter.

Hurst couldn't see if they were near the jetty with the moored rowing boat. His plan was disintegrating. Perishing in the hostile conditions now appeared the most likely outcome.

While the unwelcome thought crossed his mind, the intensity of the snow decreased, and in the glow thrown-up by the white landscape he could make out a jetty about 300 feet away.

Alice was now suffering badly from the bitter cold, staggering in the freezing depths and on the verge of collapse. Her father moved to support her.

"Back!" Hurst threatened with the knife, pointing it at her. Paul stopped, fearing she'd be killed. His hatred for the man ran deep, but he felt helpless to attack while his daughter was so vulnerable

Hurst ordered Paul to walk in front of him toward the jetty, while he roughly pulled the girl along. When they reached it, the fugitive was greatly relieved to see the rowing boat moored alongside, its protective canvas buried under snow.

He told Paul to remove the cover and take up position to row the boat. Then he hauled the girl on board. He knew the cottage across the water was in a half-left direction from the jetty. If the break in the snow held, he might even see its window lights to guide them as they crossed the lake.

But the weather didn't hold. Halfway across the wind intensified again, rocking the boat perilously, every pitch threatening to throw them into the violent waves. Then the snow began to thicken, destroying any hope of visibility.

Paul struggled on, hardly able to row as the wind and waves took control. He was obeying only in the hope the maniac in the boat wouldn't kill his daughter. But now he was beginning to fear she might die anyway from cold and exhaustion. Alice looked pitiful sitting beside Hurst, her small frame sunk forward over her knees, and his knife ready to act if her father tried any tricks.

The wind strength increased and Paul lost all control over the boat as it rocked and turned helplessly on the waves. Any hopes of surviving the journey were fast fading. Then suddenly they heard scraping beneath the craft. It had reached shore. But where?

Hurst ordered Paul to get out of the boat and drag it further on to the land, but his strength was ebbing away. Standing in the freezing lake waters up to his waist, he could barely move it against the force of the elements, and was in danger of being violently struck as it thrashed around.

Hurst told the girl to get out, but she could hardly move.

"For Christ's sake, let me lift her out," her father shouted. "I'm hardly likely to make a quick getaway, am I?"

Their captor consented. His victims were in no state for any heroics. Now his main concern was trying to find the cottage. Although he was a strong man, the elements and stress were taking their toll on him too.

Paul carried his daughter. She was only small, but in his weakened state, it was a struggle battling against driving snow and storm force winds.

"Where are we going?" he shouted into the lashing elements. "She'll die soon, if we can't find shelter."

Hurst ignored him. He was more concerned about himself dying from cold. It was becoming a hopeless quest.

Then they heard the distant barking of a dog. They turned to follow the sound, in the hope it would lead them to the shelter of a home. The snow was falling heavily, but after struggling further they could see window lights not far away.

Hurst had no idea if it was the cottage he had been aiming for, but it was refuge. He turned to Paul. "We'll be all right now. Put your daughter down and rest for a minute. Then we'll head for the place."

Paul was puzzled by the almost friendly tone coming from his enemy, but he needed to stop very briefly to regain strength before carrying his daughter further.

He stood Alice down, supporting the girl with his right arm. Hurst drew close and stabbed him in the stomach.

The fugitive approached the cottage. It looked welcoming. The dog barking was now muted, coming from inside the dwelling. Snow was piled high against the walls except for the front door, which had recently been opened.

Hurst knocked on it. He could hear a bolt being drawn back. Flakes of snow flew into the house as an elderly man peered out at him.

"I've been hiking. I lost my way in the blizzard," Hurst pleaded his dire situation.

"Come in, quickly," the man beckoned.

Hurst entered, clutching his travel bag and thanking his host as he stood in the hallway with snow melting off his clothes on to the floor.

"Come inside and warm yourself. Take off your coat and hang it there," the man pointed to a coat stand. He was stooping, holding a brown and white beagle dog by the collar. The creature was yelping and seemed agitated by the visitor, giving whining howls of disapproval.

"Quiet!" the owner commanded. The dog growled and obeyed.

Hurst entered the welcome warmth of the living room. Burning logs crackled in the cosy, open fireplace. He was soon greeted by an equally warming smile from a woman entering the room.

"This is my wife, Shauna," the man introduced her. She looked ten years younger than her husband, who Hurst guessed must be in his late sixties.

"And I'm Gordon. Gordon McKinley."

Hurst had no intention of relaying his real name. Thinking quickly he introduced himself.

"I'm Andy Ramsey."

They shook hands.

"Shauna was just preparing our dinner. Please join us. You must be exhausted." Gordon extended their hospitality further.

Hurst couldn't believe his luck. From the brink of disaster to the lap of luxury in the space of an hour.

"And you must change your wet clothes or you'll catch your death," Shauna advised him. "My husband will find you some of his. They might not fit, but they'll be fine until I can wash and dry yours."

"Thank you," Hurst replied, on his best behaviour. "But some food first would be great."

"Then come on through to the kitchen. We're eating there tonight," Gordon pointed the way. "And you can tell us all about your journey. The weather can suddenly turn very treacherous in these parts."

They entered the kitchen. Hurst was hardly likely to recount what had really happened. A story of fiction was forming in his mind.

Shauna began ladling piping-hot beef casserole on to plates as their guest was invited to sit at the kitchen table. He dived into the meal like a man starved.

"So what happened to you?" Gordon enquired.

Hurst finished a mouthful of food, and turned to his hosts ready to relate his prepared tale of fiction. But instead of seeing the man and woman sitting with him, he was now in the company of his mother and father. They were accompanied by Inspector George Bird, standing in the kitchen doorway.

He stared at them in horror. Then an intense wave of anger swept through him. He saw a chopping knife on the kitchen counter and leapt up to grab it.

"Get out, get out you bastards! Leave me alone!"

Hurst ran toward them, stabbing and slashing in a frenzy, attempting to utterly destroy his tormentors forever.

The spectres disappeared. As his fury subsided he became aware of a dog barking. It was Shauna and Gordon's dog. The man had put the animal in a nearby room so it wouldn't disturb their visitor.

Then Hurst saw the lacerated, bloodied bodies of the couple spread on the floor. Their faces contorted in horror. Smashed plates and food scattered around the room.

He ran into the hallway, grabbed his travel bag and coat and fled the cottage. The snow had eased, the thick cloud covering was breaking.

CHAPTER 9

A TEAM of four specially trained police officers fought their way through the vicious weather to the cottage where Hurst was staying.

They arrived to see the front door wide open and lights from the property shining into the darkness. The place was deserted.

There were a few indentations of tracks in the snow near the door, but they petered out within a few feet, covered by the sweeping winds spreading the snowfall.

They radioed back to their headquarters. The snow had ceased, but the weather forecast was for another blast of appalling conditions to arrive shortly. Search helicopters would be grounded until it had passed. For the moment the trail had literally gone cold.

Hurst headed up a hillside slope. Snow was starting to fall again. Until now he'd clung to the hope of finding a way to escape. That hope was rapidly fading. He feared it wouldn't be long before the police launched an aerial search for him.

His escape trek felt like he'd covered many miles. In reality he knew it was probably only a few.

Then, in the snowlight, he caught sight of what appeared to be a small dwelling almost completely buried in snow a short distance away. Taking weary steps, he began to approach it as fresh flakes began to strike his face.

As he grew closer to the construction, he could make out wood panelling jutting above the snow heaped around the base. Hurst didn't realise it at that moment, but he'd come across a converted shepherd's hut. It was rented to holidaymakers in better seasons of the year.

Brushing away the snow with his arm he found the door. It was locked. With all the strength he could muster, he shouldered it several times before it gave way.

There was no lighting or power, but after a few moments his eyes could see the shapes some appliances in a small kitchen area and, most welcoming of all, a room with two single beds. He dropped on to one of them, resting for a moment.

The wind outside was howling. Through a small section of window not covered by snow he could see the weather had deteriorated again.

 Hurst reached into his travel bag and took out a can of tomato soup. He pierced the can with the knife he'd used to stab Paul, then drank the contents.

He desperately wanted to rest, but feared search parties might soon be out looking for him. He laid back on the bed with the idea of just having a short nap.

When he awoke, there was dim light coming through the window. He sat up in panic. The nap had turned into a long sleep. He needed to get away. Looking out the window he saw the snow had stopped. Any tracks he left now would not be quickly covered, and ground or aerial searches of the area would spot them easily.

If the police hadn't yet discovered his cottage hideout, someone was likely to alert them to the couple he had murdered only hours before. He needed to find another place to hide. He'd have to chance leaving tracks, there was no other way.

Hurst prepared to leave when he became aware of a faint buzzing sound. He went to the front door and pulled away a chair wedged under the door handle, which had kept it shut after his break-in.

He looked out and saw a small, dark shape in the distance just above the horizon. It was a helicopter. *The police were coming!* Soon they'd be scouring the area. If he went outside now he'd be exposed. He was trapped.

The dawn light was breaking as Detective Superintendent, Susan Hopkin, and Sergeant Dan Glover, exited the helicopter which touched down near Hurst's hideaway cottage.

The D.S. had received information on route that the place was deserted and she felt bitterly disappointed. But it was a vital starting point in the pursuit of Hurst and, more importantly, trying to save Alice. Whether her father had found his way to the cottage, the superintendent had no idea, but there might be clues inside.

The two police officers entered the property and the advance search party showed them a young girl's light blue dress they'd found. It fitted the description of the dress Alice had been wearing when she was abducted.

Outside other officers were brushing away the snow covering the parked car. When D.S. Hopkin saw the vehicle, she instantly recognised it as the one Billy Parsons had sold to Hurst. The suspect had definitely been at the cottage with the girl.

A search helicopter had been surveying the immediate area and was now crossing to the other side of the loch. It spied an empty rowing boat washed up on to the shore by the turbulent waves of the night storm.

Hopkin and her sergeant were looking around the cottage for any clues that might indicate where Hurst had gone, when a call came from the search aircraft. The crew had found two bodies in a cottage across the waters. On hearing the news Hopkin and Glover took off for the scene of carnage.

Detective Inspector, Robert McCullen, from the regional police force had also landed there by helicopter when the D.S. and Glover arrived. He was officially in charge of the operation, but had been informed that Hopkin was permitted to help in pursuing the case.

A red-haired man in his early forties, the inspector was dressed in thick clothing for the freezing weather, unlike his colleagues from the south who, in their rush to reach the scene, wore jackets and trousers that didn't offer much protection from cold.

The officers shook hands, briefly greeting each other, before entering the gruesome scene of butchery inside the cottage.

They saw Gordon and his wife Shauna on the kitchen floor, their bodies mutilated from the vicious chopping knife attack. Even for the detectives, who had witnessed some harrowing scenes, it was difficult to bear.

"My God, has he killed Alice as well?" D.S. Hopkin feared the worst.

"My officers have searched the place and haven't found her," Inspector McCullen offered a crumb of comfort.

"Then let's pray she's still alive," Sergeant Glover shook his head in disbelief as he stared at the bodies on the floor.

"Forensics are on the way. For now we'll just have to leave them resting where they are," McCullen explained.

As he finished speaking they heard a call from outside.

"Quick there's something over here!"

They rushed to the door to see a search officer beckoning them to an object in the snow a short distance away.

As they approached, the officer was kneeling beside a small mound in the snow with what looked like part of a trouser leg and black shoe protruding from it.

The officer began brushing away the cover. There were red streaks beneath the top layer. The detectives knelt down and together the team slowly revealed the body of a man laying face down. They turned it over to check if there was any sign of life. As they did so, they saw the body of a young girl nestled underneath.

Hurst was beginning to panic at the prospect of spending the rest of his life behind bars if he was caught. There seemed to be no way he could escape, trapped inside the holiday shepherd's hut.

Then an idea surfaced. It was a gamble, but it was his only hope. He reached into his travel bag and took out a phone. One he'd bought from his local market stall trader and had held in reserve for an emergency.

He turned it on hoping it would pick up a signal. The battery was low with no signal showing. He grew ever more fearful as the sound of the helicopter grew louder. The police would be certain to search his hideout.

The phone flashed a warning the battery was soon to power out when a faint signal emerged. He dialled the emergency services. A woman answered.

" I'm Edwin Hurst and I want to give myself up," he told her. "There's a police manhunt for me and I'm in St Michael's Church at Drumillan." He hung up, hoping his message had got through.

Hurst guessed mobile calls in the region were probably being monitored, but it would take a little time for the authorities to nail the exact location of his call. He'd seen St Michael's Church at Drumillan on the internet when he'd been searching at the library for a hideaway in the Scottish Highlands. It was featured as one of the area's local historic features, about ten miles from the cottage he had rented.

He prayed it would act as a distraction to draw away the immediate hunt so he could break cover and find another way of escape.

The helicopter was flying closer to the shepherd's hut. Would his call get through in time to redirect his hunters? Would they believe it?

Hurst took wads of cash from his travel bag and stuffed them into the inside pockets of his coat. If he could get away, he'd abandon the travel bag. It was too cumbersome.

The copter was now hovering near the hut, the deafening sound of the rotors furiously approaching. It was beginning to descend. Hurst took hold of his knife. He did not plan to be taken easily.

Snow scattered wildly through the air as the craft was about to touch down. Suddenly its rotors roared into new life. Hurst peered cautiously out of the window to watch it rapidly ascend again, then swiftly head away.

His message must have got through. The police were heading for Drumillan. There wasn't much time. He needed to somehow find a new place of refuge as quickly as possible.

Now it had stopped snowing, it was impossible to hide his tracks and the search team would soon be back in the area when they realised they'd been duped.

Hurst left the hut, but the deep snow considerably slowed his progress. After trekking for half-an-hour he could see a woodland on a rising slope about a mile ahead, the white treetops shining crisply in the rising sunlight. It would take an age to get there for cover. The helicopter was more than likely to return before that.

As the fugitive began to climb the slope, he caught sight of a track further round the incline on his left. The snow was banked steeply on its sides. The storm force winds must have swept down it, leaving a passable path along its route. Then Hurst saw a black Land Rover in the distance driving down the track. He ran as best he could to try and reach it. Here was the possibility of escape.

He reached the edge of the track and slipped, tumbling down the snowdrift piled at its side. Struggling to gain balance on the ice, he managed to stand up again just as the vehicle approached. He waved his arms for it to stop. The driver applied the brakes, sliding to a halt. A man opened the window.

"Please help me!" Hurst began. "I've been out walking and got caught in the snowstorm."

The driver reached across and opened the passenger door. Hurst gratefully climbed in.

"You're lucky to be alive," the man greeted him.

Hurst struck out with his knife and stabbed him in the chest. The rescuer stared at him in amazement, blood rapidly oozing into his dark green sweater. Then he slumped, lifeless.

The killer reached across, opened the driver door and shoved his victim out into the snow. Quickly he clambered over to the driving seat and set off.

From time to time the vehicle slid precariously on ice and valuable time was lost as he struggled to keep it from swinging sideways and careering out of control.

After half-an-hour, he spied a highway ahead with cars able to travel on it. Snow ploughs had been at work to open a route leading to a major road. He was descending from mountainous terrain and the snow level was beginning to decrease.

Hurst estimated that the search team by now would probably have discovered he wasn't at St Michael's Church and be hard on his tail again.

If he joined the passing traffic ahead, he'd be able to confuse the search and make some headway out of the area, before the unfortunate owner of the vehicle was discovered and the details broadcast.

The cleaning lady at St Michael's Church literally had the fear of God put into her, as she lifted the cross on the altar to give it a polish.

Three police officers burst into the nave with sub-machine guns poised to fire, shouting a command for all present to remain totally still.

The elderly woman turned to see them and dropped the cross in abject horror. She collapsed in shock. No-one else was present in the building.

Detectives Hopkin and McCullen were furious that they'd been so easily sidetracked by Hurst. Of course they should have realised the phone call could be a trick, but they were so keyed up with pursuit, sense had briefly taken a back seat. Their superiors would not be happy either.

A helicopter immediately returned and landed near the shepherd's hut. It was apparent the holiday let had been broken into and used for refuge, but the bird had flown. Scouring the area again, the copter team spied a body on a track below and descended. The man was dead. Stabbed with a vicious knife wound in the chest.

There were vehicle tracks in the snow. They guessed what may have happened, but it could take a while to trace the identity of the deceased and the vehicle they were looking for.

Hurst had been travelling for two hours. Twenty miles from his escape, the roads had become much clearer, hardly touched by snow. He was on the motorway heading south and saw a service station ahead. Time for yet another change of plan. The police would trace his vehicle very soon he guessed.

He pulled into the service area and parked the car, noticing there were two CCTV cameras perched high on posts.

On the back seat of the Land Rover lay a dark green, fur-lined coat with a hood. The coat was a tight fit for him, but he put it on and pulled the hood over his head.

The police would eventually get images of the vehicle, but they wouldn't immediately see the driver had been Hurst, if he covered himself he hoped. He had no alternative.

He made his way across to the parking area for long-haul trucks and picked out the ones with overseas licence plates. A driver was walking toward one of them.

Hurst was gambling that a foreign driver would only have spent a short time delivering goods in the country before returning to Dover seaport for the ferry crossing back to the continent. The chances of him being unaware of the police manhunt were high.

The fugitive struck lucky. With hand gestures and pointing, interspersed with some broken English negotiations, the driver agreed to give him a lift. The clincher sealing the deal was a handful of notes counted to £500.

The route the driver was taking to Dover would pass within fifteen miles of Hurst's target destination. From there, with the hood up and increasing beard growth beginning to disguise his appearance, he could make his way incognito on buses.

It was a shock as Paul Hunter opened his eyes. For a moment his mind struggled to register why he was laying on a bed.

Two people were sitting beside him. They looked concerned and then began to smile. Slowly he realised it was his wife, Diane, and daughter Rosemary. They had travelled to Scotland, where Paul was being treated in Edinburgh's general hospital after being flown from the Highlands by helicopter.

He tried to sit up, but pain seared through his stomach.

"Careful! You must lie still," Diane rose from her chair in alarm, ready to help if necessary.

The memory of those harrowing moments in the snow suddenly flooded Paul's mind.

"Alice! Where is she?" Panic gripped him. He tried unsuccessfully to move again.

"It's all right, she's safe," Diane reassured him. "She's resting in a ward down the corridor. She'll be fine the doctor says."

Paul felt immensely relieved and rested his head back on the pillow, tired from the merest exertion.

"Daddy, I'm so glad you and Alice are alive," his daughter Rosemary stood and leaned over to kiss him.

"And I'm so glad to see you," Paul replied, smiling with tears of happiness beginning to trickle from his eyes, knowing his family was safe.

"I've been very stupid, haven't I?" Paul looked at his wife.

Diane could not disagree. And when she realised her husband had decided to take matters into his own hands, she'd been both furious and terrified.

But it had happened. She couldn't change it. And she couldn't help admiring Paul's heroic act in saving their daughter.

When the search team found him buried in the snow, and pulled him back to discover his daughter Alice underneath, they initially thought both were dead. But the cold had helped to slow the blood flow from Paul's stab wound.

Hurst had left him for dead after knifing him. But Paul had managed to get up again and stagger toward Alice, who in a dangerously exhausted state had collapsed at seeing her father attacked. He laid down on top of the girl to protect her from the freezing temperature.

The ensuing snowfall cover insulated them just enough to keep both alive before being discovered and flown to hospital in Edinburgh. Fortunately, the stab wound had not penetrated any vital organs or arteries, although the injury would take a few months to heal. Alice had suffered mild hypothermia and nutrition deficiency, but she too was well on the way to physical recovery. However, she would need support to help her come to terms with the terror of her dreadful experience.

There was other news that was not welcome.

Paul had noticed his left foot was protruding from the bedcover and heavily bandaged. While he and Alice were sealed by the layer of snow, his left foot had remained exposed. The result was frostbite, and three of his toes had needed to be amputated.

Hurst was also still on the loose. The house he'd settled into since escaping from Scotland was heaven compared to the hell he'd experienced two weeks earlier. A comfortable bed, all the mod cons and good food.

The only drawback was being confined to the premises, but hopefully that wouldn't last long.

He knew when he'd stepped off the bus after his flight from Scotland that he needed to act swiftly. He couldn't make calls for help by phone or internet, because the police would be monitoring everyone who was known to him. But his new destination was only a short distance away.

As Billy Parsons returned to the office at his car sales premises, he was surprised to see someone sitting at his desk. It took him a moment to see through the beard growth of the occupant.

He froze in horror. "Every fucking police force in the country is after you! What the hell are you doing here?"

Hurst ignored the less than friendly greeting from his ex-cellmate.

"I need a bit of help," Hurst understated the position.

Billy backed away, raising his hands in a gesture of defence against any involvement. "The police have been sniffing round here. They might be watching now."

""That's all right," Hurst reassured him, "I sent them off on a distraction. There's a phone box down the road. I made a hoax call to say there was a bomb in Bigdeals supermarket, a mile away. They're all down there."

Billy had wondered what was the cause of the emergency sirens he'd heard a short time ago.

"I don't mind bending a few rules – but murder, child abduction, that is way out of my league," Billy reasoned. "I'd probably get ten years just for talking to you now. I'm sorry mate, but you're on your own. Anyway, you attacked me and stole a car off me. I've done my bit for you."

Hurst continued to ignore the car salesman's protests.

"You've got a nice place in Surrey, haven't you. Secluded, a few acres of land. That would do me very nicely as a temporary place to stay."

Billy shook his head at the suggestion, ruling out any possibility of refuge there.

Hurst knew from a conversation he'd had with Billy, when they'd been in prison together, that the businessman had bought a second home in the Surrey village of Thornhill. It was off the beaten track, surrounded by high hedges and an ideal place to bury yourself away for a while. That's how Billy had described it to him.

He'd bought the property for cash in the name of his wife's cousin, as part of a tax evasion dodge on his business. Nothing official linked Billy. The deal had meant a considerable saving and investment.

The beauty of it, so far as Hurst was concerned, lay in the property having no immediate connection to Billy. So long as he stayed away from the house while Hurst was there, the police would not be alerted to it.

"But I've planned to go down there for the weekend with my wife," Billy protested.

"Change your plan," came the reply.

"Look, you know I'd like to help you, but I just can't afford to..."

"Shut up!" Hurst interrupted.

He stood up from the chair and reached into his coat pocket to produce a knife. He didn't point it, but the presence of the weapon was enough.

"If you don't help me Billy, I swear whatever happens, I will find a way to kill you and your family."

The car dealer could see the pure evil emanating from the eyes of the man facing him. He believed every word.

Billy arranged for one of his workshop engineers to drive Hurst to the house in Surrey. The employee had no idea he was driving the most reviled villain in Britain. Even if he had known, he was a discreet worker, benefiting well from the Parsons business.

He stopped on the way to buy a good supply of food from a supermarket. It would keep Hurst going for some time.

D.S. Hopkin was back on home territory after the fruitless search for Hurst had come to an end in the Scottish Highlands.

A new media push for any sightings or information about Hurst once again resulted in a big response from the public, but follow-up enquiries gave no trace to his location.

The Land Rover he'd abandoned at the motorway service area was discovered after local staff saw the vehicle description on a television news bulletin.

It was conclusive the fugitive had made his escape in it, because DNA samples and fingerprints taken from the vehicle matched his records.

Forensics also had strong evidence to prove he was responsible for the murder of the unfortunate couple in the cottage as well as the Land Rover driver, a local farmer. However, the murder weapon was missing and the hope of another lead had been dashed.

CCTV footage, taken from the motorway service area where Hurst had organised a lift, recorded the licence plate of the overseas driver. The police had picked up the truck's route down the motorway, but camera coverage was patchy. Nothing was recorded showing at which point the driver had dropped him off.

The truck's origin was traced to the Baltic country of Latvia. But that had also drawn a blank. The police were happy to help, but the driver had quit his job shortly after returning home. Despite public appeals, no-one knew his location.

D.S. Hopkin had calculated that Hurst would likely have returned to home territory. She traced people who'd previously known him, but they hadn't been in touch for a long time. Hurst tended to lead a solitary existence.

Of course, Billy Parsons had been at the top of her list to visit. He was a fixer and could help friends in many legal and illegal ways.

But she relied on the fact he was a middle level villain, and not one to get involved with killers and top league criminals. He wouldn't want to be implicated in murder, though Hurst might have contacted him in desperation for more transport.

However, the detective had no idea of Billy's second-home retreat, or the threat of death that hung over him and his family if he didn't comply with Hurst's bidding. In those drastic circumstances Billy's mouth was closed.

"He hasn't been here," he told Hopkin. His eyes shifted unsteadily when he was lying, but on this occasion they remained firmly fixed on the detective's own searching gaze.

For good measure she instigated a search of the car sales premises, not believing they'd find Hurst hiding there, but to pressure Billy. To let him know the authorities wouldn't tolerate him doing business with their prime murder and abduction suspect.

"If I find you've been helping him, you know what's coming," Hopkin pointed a finger of warning as she stood with detective, Dan Glover, in the car sales office.

Billy felt like a schoolboy who'd been given a final chance before stronger action would follow. Except punishment in this case wouldn't be just the loss of playtime.

Hurst was growing restless. Although he was grateful for the hideout in Billy's second-home, the plan they had hatched together was nearly ready to execute.

Billy communicated with Hurst through a trusted intermediary, John Paxton, his car sales manager. He was a big man in his late thirties who always presented well in smart, fashionable suits. He had also served time for petty crime. Paxton was additionally useful in dealing with awkward buyers who looked like causing trouble with 'silly' complaints about their purchases.

He never travelled directly from the used car premises to see Hurst at the Surrey home, because he and Billy were aware the police were probably surveilling employee activity. He usually took a roundabout route.

It involved Paxton driving a car from work dressed in a mechanic's overall and wearing a woolly hat drawn over his forehead. He would take the vehicle to a local associate's car repair workshop and once inside swap cars.

Half-an-hour later, a real mechanic wearing a woolly hat would drive the car in which Paxton had arrived back to Billy's. Any police surveillance would not be able to see the car was being returned by a substitute driver. It gave the appearance of the vehicle just going into the workshop for a check-up.

Paxton would then leave the workshop in a different car to head for Hurst's hideaway. He knew the man he met there was on the run from the authorities. But Hurst's changed appearance, with a beard and different clothing, left him unaware of the fugitive's infamous identity.

Even if he had known, Paxton would have been happy to carry out Billy's secret bidding through loyalty. The businessman had given him a well paid job after he'd suffered much rejection from other employers because of his prison record for bank robbery.

In the weeks of hiding, Hurst had hatched a plan with Billy Parsons to escape abroad using the go-between.

Billy had made a business connection in the past with a man in Italy who imported high class stolen cars to order from locations around Europe. It was in a higher league than Parsons' normal level of crime. But he acted as a well paid intermediary with UK contacts who supplied the required vehicles.

The Italian, Alberto Rossini, was a wealthy man and owned a large country estate in Tuscany that required day to day upkeep. Rossini was seeking a new assistant to work on the estate, maintaining his swimming pool, repairing and decorating his buildings and keeping the grounds and gardens in good order.

Because of the nature of their business, Billy and Rossini communicated with different identities across the internet and through third parties using scrambled messages.

Billy persuaded Rossini to take on Hurst as his new assistant. No, he didn't speak Italian, but as a labourer that would not be a problem. The estates manager handled the everyday office business.

Hurst had carried desires to rise above being a lowly labourer, but present circumstances offered him little other choice.

The plan involved smuggling him out of the UK as a crew member on a private yacht, owned by a business partner of Rossini, which was currently moored on the south coast at Poole harbour in Dorset.

For Rossini the deal meant cheap labour on his estate. For Billy it was costly. The risk of smuggling out a wanted man clocked a £30,000 fee for the Italian. But Billy was happy at the prospect of removing Hurst from his life forever.

Detective Susan Hopkin was at home in her two-bedroomed flat, undressing and getting ready for bed. It had been a long day.

As well as the hunt for Hurst, she had become involved with the search for a man suspected of shooting a rival drug dealer outside a club. Once again enquiries were leading nowhere. She needed a break.

Sometimes she wished she had someone close to confide in. But her career had taken precedence over her life. She'd had a relationship with two men over the years, deeply felt. A lifetime's commitment, however, did not appeal. Except at times of reflection like this. When nothing seemed to be going right.

She showered, then climbed into bed about to switch off the bedside lamp. The phone rang. She answered.

"I think we may have found a lead in the Edwin Hurst case," a night duty detective informed her.

Another week passed and John Paxton was briefed on the final run to the fugitive holed up in Billy's country home – his mission to deliver falsified documents giving Hurst a new identity.

That evening a driver employed by Rossini's business associate would take him to the yacht bound for Italy.

Paxton carried out the usual change of clothes and car swap routine at the workshop and set off.

An hour later he pulled up on the hideout driveway. For a moment the go-between sat admiring the neatly cut lawns surrounding the five-bedroomed property, its white walls gleaming in the sunlight, topped by red roof tiles. He dreamt that one day he'd have enough money, like his employer, to buy a grand house with grounds.

Paxton climbed out of the car, walked to the front door and rang the doorbell. There was no reply. He looked through a front window, but couldn't see Hurst. Perhaps he was upstairs and hadn't heard the doorbell ring.

He took a set of keys from his overall pocket and unlocked the front door. He was becoming concerned. Hurst usually waited a moment to be sure his visitor was alone before answering, but this was longer than normal.

Paxton entered the house. All was quiet in the hallway. The coat stand usually had Hurst's brown parka hanging on it. But the coat wasn't there.

The messenger looked up the stairway. Was Hurst in one of the rooms? Then Paxton caught sight of a slip of paper on the hall table. There was writing on it. He picked up the note and read: *Give me a call.*

Hurst had insisted on having a mobile phone. Not for general use, but in the event of an emergency. He had written the number on the note.

Paxton reached for his mobile – and was struck by terror.

"Get on the floor!" A man screamed from behind. "Face down! Spread your arms!"

Instinctively Paxton looked back to see an armed police officer pointing a semi-automatic rifle at him.

He obeyed instantly.

Within seconds more armed officers poured into the property, mounting the stairs, searching the house ready to shoot. But apart from the go-between the place was empty.

D.S. Hopkin was stationed outside with armed police ready to spring into action if Hurst tried to escape. Other officers were surrounding the grounds.

The detective's disappointment at not capturing her quarry was deep. She really believed this time she'd nailed him.

"He's more cunning than a fox," she remarked to her detective sergeant, who was holding a hand gun ready to act in the event of necessity.

"A fucking psychopathic bastard," Glover replied in plainer language. He was furious at not being able to lift the killer from circulation.

Their lead to the house had come from a trawl through Billy Parsons' bank account.

A huge sum of two million pounds had been transferred from it to another account.

Enquiries led to a man called Andrew Simpson, who turned out to be the cousin of Billy's wife. It was not difficult to make him admit the purpose was to launder money and evade tax on the purchase of Parsons' second home. The cousin didn't want any involvement with murder charges.

Surveillance was immediately stepped up, and the vehicle leaving the workshop of Billy's car repair associate, driven by disguised Paxton, was picked up on CCTV heading on roads towards Parsons' other home.

For D.S. Hopkin it was the clincher. Hurst was hiding there. But she wanted to catch the whole criminal chain involved with allowing the vile killer to escape.

Now she realised her delay in moving swiftly had given him yet another chance to evade justice.

She entered the house. Hurst's note was on the floor beside face-down Paxton. He was ordered to stand up and searched for weapons.

Hopkin looked at him, wanting to spit at someone who would stoop so low as to help a murderer and child abductor.

"I'm just a messenger for Billy Parsons, I don't know what this is all about," Paxton pleaded, distraught and terrified. But the detective wasn't moved by his snivelling.

She picked up the note on the hall floor and read the message.

"Hurst wrote this, didn't he?" she looked at her prisoner. He nodded.

"Ring the number," she ordered him.

It occurred to her that Hurst was playing safe and would answer the call.

"Ask him why he isn't here. Act naturally. Tell him it's safe."

Paxton keyed the number.

Hurst answered. "Are the police there?"

The question threw the caller totally off-guard. He faltered.

"No...the coast is clear," Paxton didn't sound convincing He was shaking. Hurst hung up.

The fugitive was in a car parked two miles away. It was Billy's vehicle. A silver BMW that Hurst had seen in the garage. He'd found the keys on a hook in the kitchen.

He had an uneasy feeling the police were keeping a close eye on Parsons' contacts. He wanted to be sure the go-between wasn't being followed. Now the whole plan was fucked.

The police had tracked his hideout. It was obvious from Paxton's tone in the phone call that he was shaking with nerves. Hurst knew, from his own experience, how the voice betrayed composure when they put you under the screws.

And who was to blame? That interfering bastard who'd bought his house. The anger inside bubbled like a fomenting volcano.

Hurst had seen on television and read in the papers the stories about the remarkable rescue of Paul Hunter and his daughter Alice in the Scottish Highlands. Now he deeply regretted he hadn't just killed both of them at the holiday cottage when he had the chance.

But if he was going to go down, he'd take someone from Hunter's family with him.

He started the car and edged out into the traffic from the lay-by where he'd parked. Revenge now entirely clouded his mind. His lifeline for escape had been cut away.

Hurst made the journey to the home of Paul Hunter's in-laws where his wife, Diane, and their daughters had been staying. He had no idea if they were still living there. It didn't matter. If he killed the grandparents alone, the family would suffer.

He parked the car near the same spot where he'd abducted Alice.

Diane and her parents were sitting at the kitchen table enjoying coffee together. She was excited about a sales offer she and Paul had received for the accursed property they'd bought from Hurst. The one to which she vowed never to return.

"Paul and I thought the rumours about it being haunted would put people off," Diane explained to her parents, "but it actually attracted more interest."

Paul was working upstairs in the spare bedroom set up as a temporary office. After losing three toes on his left foot due to frostbite, his wife had insisted he remained with them while recuperating. The loss had also temporarily affected his walking balance.

He was happy to comply, because living and working alone in the house they planned to sell had become an increasingly eerie experience.

But things were now looking up. Paul's notoriety, gained in the media, had turned out to be great publicity, attracting more clients for his new business.

The downside was how the dreadful episode had affected the couple's daughters. They were receiving counselling to help them cope with the trauma that had suddenly been heaped on their young lives.

Conversely, the episode was more difficult for Rosemary to come to terms with than Alice. Rosemary's fear of losing her sister had struck deep.

Presently they were staying with Diane's sister who lived in a small village on the North Wales coast. The children knew their auntie Edith and family well, and were happier away from surroundings that carried distraught memories.

Diane and Paul missed them, but were in frequent contact and grateful their girls were gradually getting better. And while Hurst was still on the loose, they thought it best for them to be somewhere he didn't know about.

A police support officer was no longer stationed at the house, but the family had been given a direct number to call in the event of Hurst showing up.

Diane sipped her coffee at the kitchen table and described to her parents some of the houses she and Paul had been viewing as prospects for their new home. The doorbell rang.

It didn't take D.S. Hopkin long to extract from John Paxton that he was the go-between for Parsons and Hurst.

The man was still shaking as he handed over to Hopkin the false identity papers meant for the fugitive. She arranged for a team to move in on Billy's premises and arrest him. She was also trying to get a phone location trace of Hurst's hiding place when he answered Paxton's call. Once again he'd been one step ahead. But now his options for escape were narrowing.

The Poole harbour police had also been notified to prevent the yacht bound for Italy from sailing, and to arrest the owner and crew.

D.S. Hopkin feared Hurst had yet another plan up his sleeve to disappear. For all his failings, he was not short on cunning.

While officers searched Parsons' house and grounds for any clues that might show where the fugitive was heading, it occurred to Hopkin she should call Paul Hunter and his family.

The grandparents' house, where they were staying, was only an hour's drive away. Hurst was most likely, she thought, to be getting as far away as possible. But it wouldn't hurt to let them know they should be careful, and immediately call the direct line if they suspected he was in the area.

As Hopkin and her detective sergeant accompanied John Paxton in the police car back to headquarters, she was starting to grow anxious.

Earlier she had rung both Paul and his wife, but neither had replied. She told herself all was probably well.

However, she decided to contact the local police in their area and ask an officer to pay them a visit. Just to make sure they were safe.

The chime of the doorbell faded as Diane got up from her chair in the kitchen to answer the call. She engaged the security chain and looked through the spyhole before opening the door. She could see the short pathway to the garden gate, but no-one was visible.

It's the postman, she thought, *he can never wait.*

She was expecting a parcel delivery. *He's probably next door to see if he can leave it there.*

Diane took off the security chain and started to open the door. Hurst swiftly shot out from the side of the doorway and booted it open. The impact sent Diane sprawling backwards on to the floor.

He entered, pointing a knife at her. He slammed the front door shut.

Paul was upstairs, about to answer his ringing phone, when he heard the door slam. He got up to investigate. He limped, still adjusting to the loss of his toes. He looked over the bannister to see his wife laying on the hall floor and Hurst holding a knife.

"Diane!" he yelled in horror fearing she'd been stabbed. Like lightning he leapt down the stairs to help her. But his unsteady foot slipped and he tumbled, cracking his head on the tiled floor below. He lay motionless.

"Paul!" his wife screamed, rising to his aid.

"Shut up! Get back!" Hurst threatened with the knife.

"But I've got to help him," she pleaded.

Diane's parents had come to the kitchen door, wondering what was causing the commotion. Hurst saw them.

He grabbed Diane by the arm, twisting it behind her back and holding the sharp blade of the knife to her throat.

"Get in there!" Hurst nodded toward an open doorway leading to the living room.

Diane's parents looked horrified but obeyed, dreading the intruder might slit their daughter's throat. They didn't recognise the man. They'd never seen him in the flesh. His beard growth made him look different to the media publicity photos. But it didn't take them a leap of imagination to know who he was.

They entered the room as Hurst followed with Diane, keeping the knife dangerously close to her throat.

"Where are the kids?" Hurst demanded.

"They're not here," Diane's father told him.

"Where are they?" Hurst's eyes were bulging with fury.

In his deranged state, he had it in mind to abduct them both, so he could keep the police at bay with threats of violence if his wishes for an escape route were not met.

"They're in police protection," Diane's mother answered, trembling, trying to keep a firm grip on the fear that was starting to tear her apart inside.

There was an awful silence as Hurst assessed whether the woman was telling the truth. He thought if the children were in the house, they would probably have appeared by now to see what the noise was about. And it was possible the police would be keeping them in protective accommodation while he was still free.

Hurst satisfied himself that the girls' grandmother was probably telling the truth. A change of plan was required.

"You'll have to do then," he snarled at Diane. But before he escaped with his alternative hostage, he intended to plunge his knife into the heart of the unconscious bastard on the hall floor. The man he blamed for all his present ills.

A police patrol car pulled up outside the house. An officer got out of the vehicle while his driver colleague remained.

All looked peaceful, so it probably needed only a quick check to make sure all was well in the household. The officer rang the doorbell. He waited, but there was no reply. He radioed his headquarters and the message was relayed to detective Hopkin.

"They're probably out shopping or something," the patrol-man told her. "Nothing here to indicate any problem."

"Check to see if there's a silver BMW car there," Hopkin instructed, giving him details of the vehicle which she'd obtained from a terrified Billy Parsons who was now in custody.

The officer in the police car was listening to the conversation on his radio. He climbed out and started walking down the road, checking the parked vehicles. He stopped in his tracks the second he saw the one described. Quickly he joined his colleague.

They checked round the back of the house. All was silent. They noticed all the curtains were drawn closed and radioed back to the detective superintendent.

"Don't attempt to gain access," Hopkin commanded, "unless you see any immediate cause to help. I'm sending in armed back-up."

It was a difficult decision for her to make. Hurst could be inside the house murdering the family at this moment. On the other hand they could be alive, and any botched attempt at entry could seal their death. Expert help was needed.

"Just keep the house under surveillance," she cut off.

Twenty minutes later a team of armed officers arrived. They were instructed to take up positions surrounding the house, but not to launch an assault.

Five minutes later D.S. Hopkin arrived with her detective sergeant. She tried again to contact Paul on his phone. This time it was answered.

"Hello Paul. It's Susan Hopkin..." she began.

"If you try and break-in here, the family is dead!" Hurst threatened.

Hopkin was about to reply, but the connection cut off.

Hurst had peered through a small opening in the curtains and seen a police presence at the front of the house. He knew from the television news that a detective superintendent called Susan Hopkin was heading the hunt for him. He was obviously trapped.

Hopkin removed a loud hailer from the boot of the police car and called toward the house.

"Edwin Hurst. We know you've had a difficult time." She was trying the ploy of sympathy to try and exploit his sense of self-pity.

"If you give yourself up now, we'll do our best to help you," she hoped the compromise might lead him to surrender.

But the plea fell on deaf ears.

Hurst continued to hold the knife at Diane's throat. If the police got hold of him, he was going to spend the rest of his life in prison. There was really nothing else to lose. He forced Diane toward the window in the front room and made her partly draw back the closed curtain.

Hopkin saw them standing there, the knife across Diane's throat. One of the armed officers trained his rifle at the window ready to take out the target, but Hurst was keeping behind his victim. Any shot would kill Diane. Hurst told her to open the window a few inches.

"I want you to withdraw your armed men and arrange for a jet to fly me to Chile," he shouted through the opening. "And I want a loaded gun posted through the door. Any tricks and I'll kill this woman and the rest of her family."

Diane shut the window at Hurst's command and closed the curtain again.

It was a ludicrous request. Hopkin couldn't possibly arrange Hurst's escape or arm him with a weapon. But she couldn't allow him to murder the family either. Not that she knew for sure if there were any other family members present in the house. She was aware, however, that the children were a long distance away, staying with their aunt and uncle. That at least was a great relief.

The fact he wanted a gun, also indicated he was armed only with a knife. He could be bluffing, but she'd have to take the chance. In the rush to get to the scene there had been no time for her collect bulletproof clothing.

The detective called through the loud hailer again.

"I'm Detective Superintendent, Susan Hopkin. Let me come in and speak to you. We can work something out." Now it was a gamble with her own life if he agreed.

Hurst was uncertain. It could be a trick, but he might be able to negotiate his way out with a face to face meeting.

He had made Diane's parents tie their son-in-law's arms and legs with dressing gown cords while he was still unconscious in the hall. Then he had ordered them to lay face down on the living room floor.

Hurst saw the old couple as a liability. They might try to tackle him while he was distracted. Diane begged her captor to let them go, but to no avail. He had no time to tie them up. He eyed the sofa.

"I'm releasing you for a moment," he told Diane, "one move out of place and I'll kill them," Hurst indicated her parents.

Continuing to hold the knife, he stooped and with his free hand gripped the bottom edge of the sofa, hauling it toward the elderly couple, who were still face down on the floor. He drew it over their legs then lowered the base, trapping them underneath.

They cried in pain as the full weight of the furniture descended. Hurst was satisfied it would prevent them from making any quick attempts at escape or attack.

Diane instinctively moved to help them. Hurst hit her in the face, dazing his hostage for a moment, giving him enough time to grip her in an arm-lock and place the knife at her throat. Then he shoved Diane toward the window, ordering her to open it.

An armed police officer had taken up position in the second-floor bedroom of the house across the road to gain better aim if Hurst came to the window again.

But the fugitive was well aware that the enemy would be ready to take a shot at him given the slightest chance.

This time he lowered himself behind Diane, pressing the knife point on her left kidney. She winced as Hurst made a small puncture in her flesh. She knew he would drive it in there, and elsewhere on her body, if she disobeyed.

"Tell that woman Hopkin I'll let her inside, but any tricks and you're all dead," he ordered Diane.

She shouted the message.

"Unarmed, she has to be unarmed," Hurst added. Diane conveyed the terms.

The armed officer in the bedroom was unable to get the target in his sights. Now it was all down to the detective superintendent as she waited beside a police car with Sergeant Glover.

He offered to take on the role for her. She thanked him, but declined.

"Oh no. I want to get this little bastard," she replied, starting to walk down the path to the house.

Continuing to hold the knife at Diane, Hurst pushed her into the hall where Paul still lay unconscious on the floor bound by the dressing gown cords.

Hurst could see through the pane of frosted glass in the front door that someone was standing outside.

"Any tricks and she gets it," he shouted.

"I'm alone, unarmed," the detective called back.

"Open it," Hurst ordered Diane. She reached out and began to open the door.

"Stop!" Hurst commanded, pulling Diane back before it had fully opened. He wanted a distance between him and the detective.

On his order, Hopkin entered and closed the door behind her.

"Get your jacket and top off," Hurst demanded.

The officer hesitated.

"I'm unarmed," she insisted.

Hurst placed the knife blade on Diane's throat.

"Okay."

Hopkin removed the clothing.

"Now your skirt."

She reluctantly obeyed, and began to wonder if the criminal had another agenda to sexually assault her or even worse. She stood there in her black bra and panties feeling entirely defenceless.

Hurst sensed her concern.

"You must be bloody joking. I wouldn't *touch* a copper, let alone..." his sentence died away.

He'd felt a pang of desire as she undressed, but his hatred of the police and authority was a far greater passion.

"Get in there," he waved Hopkin toward the living room with the knife and followed with his hostage.

Paul was face down on the hall floor and beginning to regain consciousness. He ached and attempted to move, becoming aware that his arms and legs were bound. Then sound began to penetrate his mind and the memory of losing balance and toppling down the stairs.

That voice! That dreaded voice! He could hear Hurst talking in the living room. *My God! He's in the house.*

Paul struggled trying to free himself from the dressing gown cords. His arms were tied behind his back.

"I want a jet to fly me to Chile," Hurst repeated his ludicrous demand to the superintendent, "and all armed police outside to leave."

The officer knew she could never accede to his terms, but she needed to stall him while the team outside could organise an expert force to storm the house and disarm him.

"I can arrange that for you," she lied, "but it will take a bit of time."

Paul was fortunate that his father-in-law had been ordered to tie him up. He'd made the knot look firm without it being too tight. Hurst hadn't examined it closely while all the other distractions were taking place. After more struggling the bond was loosening.

"If you could just take the knife away from Diane's throat and release her, you can have me as a hostage instead," Hopkin tried to reason with their captor.

As she spoke, Hurst began to stare at her in horror. Instead of seeing Hopkin standing there, it was Detective Inspector, George Bird. The man he had murdered and consigned to the bottom of the lake.

The officer was shaking his head disapprovingly. He raised his arm and pointed a finger as if to say 'I'm going to get you'.

Hurst pushed Diane aside and lunged the knife at his dead nemesis.

D.S. Hopkin dodged to her right, but the blade penetrated her stomach. She staggered and fell. Pain and confusion swept through her. Why had Hurst suddenly attacked?

Diane backed away, free of her aggressor's grip. Hopkin was struggling on her side, attempting to move across the floor, blood streaming from her wound. All Hurst could see was the dreaded inspector he thought he'd already killed. Now he would really finish the job.

Diane saw Hurst preparing to lunge again at Hopkin. She grabbed a vase off the dresser and threw it at his head.

It struck, making him recoil. Enraged he turned to Diane. Now she would pay. He leapt at her. Now free of his bonds Paul rushed into the room. Pure adrenalin drove out his foot handicap. He forcefully barged Hurst sending him flying across the room into the coffee table. The knife spun from the madman's hand as he failed to keep his balance and fell sprawling on to the floor.

He quickly scrambled up and began looking frantically around for the knife.

Paul was rounding on him. The two men met. Hurst grabbed his opponent by the throat and started to squeeze. His immense strength threatened to extinguish Paul's life in seconds.

Diane had freed her parents and now they piled into the attacker, punching and tearing at him, shouting in a wild frenzy. Their assault made Hurst loosen his grip.

Now raging, he turned and punched out in fury, sending Diane's mother crashing on to the floor. Her husband was furious. He struck Hurst in the face with his fist, but the impact hardly troubled the killer as he spied his knife on the carpet a few feet away from the injured detective.

Hopkin was crawling with difficulty trying to reach it. Hurst rushed for the weapon. The detective grabbed the knife and raised it in defence. Paul shoved the attacker hard to direct him away from the injured woman, but the blow caught Hurst off-balance and he fell toward her.

The last he remembered was searing pain as the blade entered his left side.

The doorbell rang. Paul and Diane were at home in their new house. This time the call wasn't the beginning of a vicious attack.

The visitor was D.S. Susan Hopkin. She was off-duty. Fortunately her injury had not been life threatening. A month of recuperation had enabled her to fully recover.

She was visiting the Hunter family to see how they were coping after their harrowing experiences.

The girls, Alice and Rosemary, were upstairs playing music. They'd made good progress in the months following Hurst's capture. Their life was turning around for the better. And Paul's business was starting to prosper.

For Hurst it was a different story. Retribution had come at last. He too survived physically. However, that's as far as it went.

His court trial for multiple murder and child abduction started, but had to be halted. He claimed there were ghosts in the courtroom staring at him.

Often he became violent, attempting to attack the apparitions and disrupting the hearing so that he needed to be restrained. No-one else could see the spectres of his deceased mother and father and the late inspector George

Bird. Sometimes they were behind the jury and at other times behind the judge.

The evidence of his guilt for murder while on the run was convincing, and those poor souls were at least given decent burials.

But no-one ever discovered how the detective inspector had disappeared, decaying unknown at the bottom of the lake, or his parents, minced in the quarry crusher and distributed among stones and dust. They were never honourably laid to rest.

Hurst's state of mind became increasingly unbalanced and he was committed to a secure psychiatric hospital.

His frenzied attacks grew more and more frequent, babbling and screaming at thin air, pleading for the other occupants of his cell to leave him in peace, even though no-one else was confined with him. But for Hurst they were always there, in waking and sleeping.

The authorities put him on suicide watch, though he would never take his own life. He feared that when he died, the ghosts would be waiting to persecute him on the other side. Pointing. Shaking their heads in disapproval. Telling him what a dreadful person he had been.

*****

HURST died five years later. At the end he was completely broken and looked like a withered old man, far in excess of his actual age.

Another five years passed before the car in which he'd disposed of the unfortunate Detective Inspector, George Bird, was discovered. It happened during an underwater search for the body of a young man who'd perished swimming in the dangerous quarry lake.

Tests on the skeleton found in the car and dental records revealed the identity of the missing officer.

The car licence plates and engine chassis number, though badly eroded, matched old records of Edwin Hurst's ownership. The mystery was solved.

But the murderer's parents were never properly laid to rest. Their pulverised earthly bodies could never be discovered.

The people who bought Hurst's former house from Paul and Diane Hunter soon moved out. There were strange occurrences. The spectres of a younger man attacking an old man and woman with a knife, and then pleading for their forgiveness. A kitchen knife curiously appearing on the counter.

The house was left unoccupied for years until a builder bought the run-down property, demolished it and constructed a new home.

But the spectres remained on that cursed spot. Never able to rest. Probably forever.

OTHER BOOKS BY THE AUTHOR

I hope you enjoyed *The Soul Screams Murder*. If you would like to read more of my stories they are listed below and available through Amazon.

As a taster, I include here the first part of my popular novel:

DARK SECRETS COTTAGE

CHAPTER 1

YOU NEVER KNOW which event is going to entirely change your life. There's usually no inkling. No clue. And so it was when a solicitor contacted me out of the blue to tell me I'd been left a cottage in the will of my great uncle, John Taverner.

I didn't know I had a great uncle, having never heard of him. I'd been adopted as a baby when my parents had died. But it didn't matter. I loved my adoptive parents dearly.

Though I did wonder from time to time who my real parents had been.

Obviously my great uncle John knew who had adopted me and where I lived, though it was a puzzle to us how, since no-one else in the family had heard of him either.

But here I was, Simon Turner, aged 35, now the proud owner of a cottage in Bursford, a small village a few miles from the South Devon coast.

At the beginning I thought it was an absolute dream, as I neared the village in my silver Fiat Punto. How could I know then, it would turn into a nightmare.

My journey to the cottage had been initially marred by a hold-up on the motorway, and I was stuck in a long queue of traffic taking me an hour-and-a-half to cover what should have taken about ten minutes. But the annoyance passed, as I departed from the mad motorway and began negotiating sharp bends on narrow country lanes, the hedgerows giving way to intermittent views of distant wooded hillsides, blurred by a blue haze.

The sun shone brightly as my heart. Everything in my life seemed to be just perfect. I'd recently been made redundant from my job as a call centre manager, which was initially quite depressing. However, the advent of my new property, coupled with a decent sum of redundancy money, now combined to give me freedom to enjoy a month in the country. To hell with it I thought, I shall leave my London flat for some relaxation and fun near the sea.

193

The satnav almost delivered me to the doorstep. It announced I had reached my destination a little short of my destination. I could see no cottage. Just high hedgerows bordering the road. Then I noticed a small track road, rutted and unsurfaced and remembered the solicitor had described it as being at the end of a very narrow, unmade road. My car would not win awards for suspension on normal roads, and as I drove along this dirt track, I feared it would shake to pieces. Fortunately, it was only for 25 metres.

The track opened on to a rectangular gravel driveway, with enough space to park about four cars. Behind stood the property, separated from the driveway by a lawn with a stone footpath to the front door. Tall hedges bordered the sides of the setting. At one time the property could probably have been described as a chocolate box cottage, complete with thatched roof. But time and neglect had now bestowed it with overgrowing weeds and cracked white render walls, ingrained with dust and dirt stains.

But I fell in love with it. Nothing some hard graft couldn't put right. I parked the car and made my way to the entrance, gravel crunching underfoot. Standing in the small, covered porch I fumbled for the front door key in my jacket pocket.

The lock was stiff but turned more easily than I'd expected, given the deep discolouring of the brass fitting. The heavy wooden door juddered slightly as I pushed it open. For a moment I sensed an atmosphere of foreboding as I glanced into the darkness of the opening, my eyes adjusting from the bright sunlight. A few feet ahead I could see a wooden staircase as I stepped inside.

Closing the door behind the sense of foreboding faded, overtaken by a feeling of pride as I looked upon my new dominion. It wasn't exactly the Ritz, more a project for one of those home makeover TV programmes, but it was mine.

A door to the right of the stairway opened into the kitchen. I flicked a light switch expecting it to be dead, but a bare bulb hanging from a cord above a pine dining table and chairs, burst into life.

The room contained a grimy gas cooker, tarnished with age and powered by a tube from a propane gas cylinder lying on the floor. A badly stained enamel sink and draining board was installed beneath a dusty sash window, which overlooked the front driveway. And a pine dresser with four drawers, beside the sink unit, completed the basic fixtures and fittings.

I turned on the cooker to see if there was any gas in the cylinder, but it was empty. However, despite the look of neglect in the room, an open grate fireplace, blackened by years of burning, gave the kitchen a cosy feeling.

A door along the hallway led to a small sitting room with considerably aged, dark wooden ceiling beams across its length. These looked attractive, but a threadbare, dark yellow sofa and matching armchair gracelessly occupied the room. At the far end, a patio door overlooked the back garden, which was overgrown with long grass and weeds.

Losing count of the number of creaks in the staircase as I ascended, I found two bedrooms with vaulted ceiling beams on the first floor, one completely empty and the other larger, main bedroom containing a metal-frame bed, bearing a battered mattress fit for the dump.

Expecting conditions to be sparse, I'd brought along some food, a sleeping bag and toiletries so I could pass the night, until I had the chance to drive to the nearby seaside town of Barcombe tomorrow and stock up on provisions.

It was irrational I know, but I had the uneasy feeling as I explored the cottage, that I was being watched. There was someone or something else present. But properties have their own particular character, especially old ones, and I put it down to that.

After the long drive down here, the motorway hold-up and a couple of refreshment breaks, it was early evening when I'd finished unpacking my things from the car.

I ate a cheese sandwich I'd brought with me, and poured a cup of lukewarm coffee from my flask. It was spartan, but I was happy. And I was heartened by the fact the place had an electricity supply with light bulbs in most of the rooms. Though I'd brought some candles, just in case.

My plan was to get an early night so I could spend some time looking around Barcombe the next day, as well as buying provisions. But before turning in, I took a stroll out the front and noticed in addition to the cracked wall render, much of the guttering was broken and parts of the roof thatch were badly worn and patchy. I was a reasonable handyman, but it appeared I'd also need some serious and expensive professional help in restoring the property to its former glory.

Feeling tired, I opted to bed down on the sitting room floor. It had a red carpet, faded and badly in need of replacement, but looking a more comfortable option for my sleeping bag than either the cold flagstone floor of the kitchen, or wooden floor-boards in the bedrooms. Sleeping on the moth-eaten mattress upstairs was totally out of the question.

By now it was dark outside. I lit a candle in the sitting room so I could see the way to my sleeping bag after turning off the main light. I plugged in my mp3 earphones and settled down, leaving the candle to burn. The warm glow was comforting, and I wasn't sure I wanted to be in complete darkness.

Thoughts of the day flashed through my mind as I made myself as comfortable as possible on the floor, and settled to my music. It was a few years since I'd bedded down in a sleeping bag. It reminded me of my boyhood and camping expeditions during the summer holidays. Truly happy times.

I awoke, aware of a sound in the cottage. The candle had gone out. It was pitch black. My earphones had dropped out, and for a second I thought it was the tinny reverberation of music still playing through them that I was hearing. I did a fingertip search for them in the darkness and picked them up. They were silent.

The sound came again. The hollow resonance of footsteps outside the room descending the wooden stairway. But I was the only person staying in the cottage. Perhaps it was an intruder, but there was nothing here of any real value to steal. I comforted myself with the thought it might be a tramp who'd found a way in at night to bed down, believing the place to be still unoccupied. I decided to get up and check.

Next second I heard what sounded like the crack of a gunshot. The sitting room door flew open. Light from the hallway streamed in. I sat bolt upright in my sleeping bag. The voices of a man and woman filled the hallway. "What the hell have you done? Jesus Christ. You'll swing for this you bastard!" It was followed by the sound of scuffling. I couldn't move with fear.

In the next moment the sitting room door slammed shut. I was in total darkness again. Silence. I could feel and hear my heart beating frantically. I remained still for several minutes, listening like a frightened animal for the slightest noise, terrified of attack. Gradually my racing heartbeat subsided. Who else was in the cottage? What was going on? I began climbing out of my sleeping bag to investigate.

As I stood up, the sitting room door opened again. This time slowly. Now there was a soft light streaming in, like a shaft of moonlight. A woman in a white nightdress with long hair trailing over her shoulders stood there. Her face was hidden in the darkness of her shadowy silhouette. She beckoned me to approach.

Continued in **DARK SECRETS COTTAGE**
by Geoffrey Sleight.

Available through Amazon or Google title search

MORE BOOKS BY THE AUTHOR

VENGEANCE ALWAYS DELIVERS

The promise of riches sets the trap for a savage revenge vendetta.

THE ANARCHY SCROLL

Dangerous quest in a land of spells and sorcery.

A GHOST TO WATCH OVER ME

A young couple discover a life threatening secret.

MORTAL TRESPASSES

Shocking revelations from a strange phone call.

THE TWIST OF DEVILS

Four unearthly tales of devils and demons.

All available on Amazon or through Google title/author search

For more information or if you have any questions
please contact me: geoffsleight@gmail.com

Or visit my Amazon Author page:
http://amazon.com/author/geoffreysleight

Twitter: http://twitter.com/resteasily

Made in the USA
Middletown, DE
21 November 2016